SHADOW OVER YESTERDAY

After a boating tragedy claims her husband's life and clouds her own memory, Paula faces a supremely difficult choice. Should she agree to marry Hugh, a popular TV personality, whose heroism in the accident and kindness since have been invaluable to her? Or should she follow the guidance of Lowell, a charismatic but controversial doctor, offering a job — and a cure — at his experimental Clinic for troubled children? Not until many ghosts are laid to rest can Paula find new happiness.

Books by Mavis Thomas
in the Linford Romance Library:

HOME IS WHERE THE HEART IS
THE SUNSHINE DAYS
BROKEN MELODY
SECOND CHANCE

MAVIS THOMAS

SHADOW OVER YESTERDAY

Complete and Unabridged

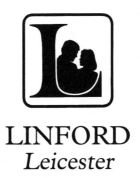

LINFORD
Leicester

First published in Great Britain

First Linford Edition
published 2003

British Library CIP Data

Thomas, Mavis
 Shadow over yesterday.—Large print ed.—
 Linford romance library
 1. Love stories
 2. Large type books
 I. Title
 823.9'14 [F]

ISBN 0–7089–9960–3

Published by
F. A. Thorpe (Publishing)
Anstey, Leicestershire

Set by Words & Graphics Ltd.
Anstey, Leicestershire
Printed and bound in Great Britain by
T. J. International Ltd., Padstow, Cornwall

This book is printed on acid-free paper

1

'No, I'm not really tired,' I told Hugh.

He was always so anxious about me. But just now, my reassurance wasn't strictly true. I was tired. This evening seemed already to have lasted for ever.

It began normally enough with two circle seats at the newest mystery play, the bright lights of London's West End reflecting on dark, wet, busy pavements — and just the usual few people recognising Hugh Egerton and excitedly proffering old envelopes to be autographed. This was something you became used to in the company of a man who was quite a public idol, his television and radio programmes high in the ratings, his books on the counters, his face looking earnestly out of magazine covers. After the theatre, we had just our usual quiet meal. The same little backwater restaurant, with

Henri hovering helpfully by our usual table.

Except that tonight it hadn't ended there. Tonight, in our candle-lit alcove, Hugh had asked me to marry him. The question I had dreaded and evaded. I didn't want to reward such great care and kindness with such deep hurt.

I was very aware of him close beside me now in the warm comfort of his car, as he drove me homewards through the spring rain. His fair, thin, sensitive face was in shadowy profile, light-coloured hair swept off his high forehead. As he turned to me momentarily, I knew his eyes would be full of concern.

'I didn't realise it was so late, Paula. Never mind, you'll soon be home. And please, don't look so worried! Can't you just let me do all the worrying from now on?'

If only I could. If my world were really that simple; instead of the confusion of elusive ghosts and half-heard echoes that had surrounded me since the tragic accident almost two years ago which shattered my life and left me no past, no memory, just emptiness.

It was impossible to put my feelings into words. I could only say, 'I was just thinking ... ' If you could call it thinking, this groping into a darkened mind.

'I know. You wouldn't be human if you didn't keep struggling to remember,' he said gently.

Guiltily I realised I was turning and turning the plain gold wedding ring on my finger. I did that very often. Hugh always stopped me when he noticed.

'Remember what that last doctor said to you, 'Live day by day, don't let the past become an obsession'?' He was rallying me in that velvet-toned voice that always so captivated his audiences.

He was right, of course. For me, the forgotten years were no real mystery, described to me often by people who loved me.

There were days long ago, I knew, when my young sister, Penny, and I, two little red-haired girls, played in a sunny country garden without a care in the world. After that, sadder days of upheaval and grief, when our mother fell ill and died very quickly, and our father took us to London to begin a new life. Although I was only four years older and shattered by my own loss; I was still like a second mother to her, Penny often told me now in her bright, bubbling, loving way.

But, when I was 18, I achieved my great ambition to become a student nurse at a big London teaching hospital. It was there I met Robert Hastings, a young, serious-faced medical student. We fell in love. A whirlwind love, a whirlwind marriage — then a harum-scarum basement flat full of medical books and lecture notes, and two goldfish called Femur and Tibia in a cracked tank.

However, I didn't finish my training right away, for a year later my son was born. Jeremy Jordan Hastings, with hair as bright as mine, with eyes as clear grey as Robert's. At least, Penny always said they were like his father's.

When Jeremy was toddling, by dint of a 'minder' and Penny's ever-ready help, I returned to nursing and eventually qualified. The following year, Robert became Dr Hastings. Oh, we were full of so many plans, Penny said.

By now, Penny herself was working as a secretary, and sharing a flat with a girlfriend. Our father had moved on to the Yorkshire branch of his farm machinery firm, and was on the point of remarrying.

But before all those fresh horizons dawned for Robert and me, we went off on the holiday we had postponed through our years of study and hasty week-end breaks. A leisurely second honeymoon along the spectacular shores of Cornwall.

One day, on the beach with Jeremy, while Robert was off on a long walk, I helped a girl who had cut her foot on some broken glass. Caroline White was a little older than me, slim and pretty, and not a little queasy at the sight of blood.

With Caroline was her fiancé, tall, fair, quietly charming, and amazingly identifiable when he removed his concealing sunglasses. It was Hugh Egerton, whose TV series 'The Friendship Hour' and 'Help Your Neighbour,' appealed for good causes. I had seen them many times. You just didn't normally find that the person dabbling in the next rockpool was someone famous, I told him, and he laughed and chatted to me, grateful for my help to Caroline.

Hearing my holiday was almost over, he insisted that tomorrow, the last day, Robert, Jeremy, and I must come on his gleaming new boat Sea Queen, to see The Giant's Teeth, the sombre Nun's Cave, and all sorts of other wonders much too good to miss.

'Of course you must all come!' Caroline said. 'I'm bringing lots of food — and a crate of sea-sick pills, aren't I, Hughie, darling?'

It was so happy a start to the day, despite a choppy sea and a scudding grey cloud or two. It was so cruel an ending. The Sea Queen developed engine trouble, then a sudden, savage storm buffeted us, and caused Caroline to fall and hurt herself badly. The disabled boat was tossed like a cork and holed upon one of the rocks along that beautiful, treacherous coast. Indeed, maybe it was merciful that those nightmare moments had been blotted from my mind!

I knew only that of the five who set out that morning, just three of us survived. Poor Caroline's body was found next day near the cave we had so admired; Robert, the clever young doctor, the beloved husband and father, perished with her.

When the freak storm passed and rescue came, only Hugh, Jeremy and I were plucked from the perilous haven of a rocky islet — chilled and exhausted, and myself barely alive after a crushing blow to my head.

There followed for me a haze of hospital wards, unreal faces, a seasaw of garish dreams and black oblivion. Afterwards, people told me I had needed two very delicate operations. My skull had been fractured and a dangerous lesion was exerting pressure on my brain. They told me as well who I was and where I was. They said the red-haired girl who wept and held my hand was my sister. They said the tall, fair man was Hugh Egerton, to whose courage I owed my life and the life of my little son.

My son! The child who shrank from me and clung to Penny.

In course of time when I was on my feet again, Hugh moved me to a luxury convalescent home on a green Surrey hilltop. I couldn't refuse because, despite his own sad loss, he devoted himself totally to me. Of course, I guessed he must feel responsible for the tragedy. He was a kind, caring, deeply sensitive man.

Eventually I went to live at Penny's

flat. Her girlfriend had married and moved out, and she had been looking after Jeremy there. I had grown already to love warm, bright little Penny dearly, as I must have loved her in the old days. I only wished it were so easy to get near the child who regarded his changed and puzzling mother with fear and dismay.

I kept the flat tidy for Penny, who had a new job and a new boyfriend called Kevin. I wrote dutifully to my father — or the grey-haired man Penny called 'Dad', who had visited me and invited me to stay at his Yorkshire home. I didn't want to do that, I wanted to be with Penny.

And all the time, of course, there was Hugh. Our relationship grew closer, and I sensed and dreaded at the same time that he planned to make me his wife. Perhaps he was really attracted to me, maybe it was because we had shared a mutual loss, but most of all, I knew he felt it his responsibility to take care of me and provide a father's guidance for Jeremy.

We had been through so much together and Hugh meant a great deal to me. Yet again and again I thought in anguish, how could I marry someone I suspected was acting mainly from a sense of duty? How could I make vows in the sight of God when I doubted if my regard for Hugh amounted to love?

'Paula, are you still with me?' Hugh was prompting beside me. These long confused daydreams always worried him. I jolted back somehow to the present.

'Yes, I'm with you! And please, don't think I haven't enjoyed this evening. It's just that I — I don't quite know how to answer what you asked me!'

As I stuttered and stammered foolishly, his hand rested briefly on my arm.

'Of course, you needn't say anything until you're ready,' he reassured me gently. 'We've all the time we need to work it all out. So, don't worry — promise me?'

I murmured, 'I promise.' But it was just to please him. I had an unnerving notion that already he was taking our joint future completely for granted.

Before much longer, we had reached the suburban backwater that was home. As usual, both kerbs were lined with a motley assortment of parked cars. Hugh cruised along seeking a place to stop until, finally, we found a space by the newly-built flats some way along.

Then, shivering in the chill and longing to get inside, yet again I found I had to share Hugh with his worshipping public. Three matronly ladies just turning in at the flats were showing all the usual symptoms. 'It is him, Vi!' 'Go on, then, you speak to him!'

Hugh looked round at them and smiled, tall, slender, grey-suited, the street lamp burnishing his hair to honey-gold. For five minutes I stood watching and listening to the scene so familiar and still so amazing to me. 'We never miss your programmes. We think you do such wonderful work. I wonder if you'd just sign your name on here?'

He spoke to them with the gentle,

charming courtesy that was unfailing whatever the hour, whatever the circumstances. He sent them on their way warmed, thrilled, glowing.

'Sorry, Paula.' Hugh was apologising to me for the delay.

'Goodness, don't be sorry. You know I — I'm happy you make people happy!' I tried to say shakily, very sincerely.

Again his hand held my arm — not patronising me, never that. He was a decade older than me. To him, what else could I ever really be but a desolate child whom he had inadvertently harmed, rescued and now must cherish in regret for always?

'Come on,' he said softly, 'let's get you inside out of the cold.'

* * *

'Well, here you both are!' Penny greeted us as my key turned in the door of one of those tall Victorian semis. 'Don't stand there in that howling draught!

Was the play any good? Oh, excuse the mess!' she exclaimed. 'Jeremy's only just in bed because we had to see the James Bond film to the bitter end!'

She gave Hugh her sparkling smile. She had never got used to having him drop in like this.

The television still flickered in its corner, surrounded by Jeremy's model spacemen and a plastic rocket ship. Some motor-bike magazines on the settee indicated Kevin Dixon's benign bearded presence there at some time during the evening.

Penny began bouncing around, clearing space to sit down; all five feet two of her, from her bobbing tail of fiery hair to her trendy denim sandals disclosing pink-enamelled toenails.

'That idiot Kev, leaving his rubbish around — he'll forget his head one day!' she grumbled.

'Or his beard?' Hugh suggested.

'No chance!' she said, giggling. 'If some big bad mugger held him up at gunpoint for his three most-prized possessions, he'd hand over his bike — he'd hand over me — but he'd fight to the death for that beard, believe me!'

Hugh laughed. Penny's brand of humour always amused him, her quicksilver nature as fast to flare up as it was to forgive and forget. Of course, people did say that in the old days I'd been far more like her than I was now. I wasn't always quiet and pale and withdrawn, so they said . . .

Tonight, to my relief, Hugh evidently didn't intend staying on a while. He had to be at the TV studio early tomorrow, he said.

At the door he promised me, 'I'll ring tomorrow.' He kissed me. I was quiet and passive in his arms. No memory of Robert stirred.

As the big car drove off, I peeped into the tiny room Penny had made into a cosy cubby-hole for Jeremy. Thankfully he was asleep, bunched up in his bed, surrounded by the largesse kind people had showered on him since the accident — books, largely unopened, toys quickly abandoned.

Wearily, I went back to Penny.

'All right, now tell me all about it! And don't pretend there's nothing going on!'

Penny, of all people, deserved not to be shut out. 'Hugh asked me to marry him,' I said simply.

'He did?' She plumped down beside me, squeezing me half-breathless in her excited embrace. 'That's wonderful! I'm so thrilled for you, Paula. I just can't tell you!'

Tears were shining in her blue eyes. In a moment, wholly unable to remain still, she was up and bouncing round the room again.

'It's the most marvellous thing! Not just because Hugh is so — well, he's out of this world, but, let's face it, he's not just awfully nice, and famous, he's rich, too!' she exulted.

'Don't look so shocked. If anyone deserves a lucky break, it's you, after all that's happened. And now you'll never have to worry again; you'll have fab holidays and a gorgeous home to come back to — and think what he'll do for Jeremy. It's a chance in a lifetime for him! Oh!' she exclaimed. 'Can I run upstairs and tell Linda and Gary? I shall burst if I don't tell someone!'

'No, please,' I begged in panic. 'Promise you won't breathe a word yet. I — I just said I'd think it over, you see.'

'You did? Well, make sure you settle it tomorrow. I can't keep quiet longer than that. If it weren't for Kev, I'd be green with envy!'

Already I had given up any thought of sharing all my torturing doubts with her. Perhaps later, when she calmed down, I might try. Even then, probably she would be unable to understand.

It was past midnight, but I had never felt less like sleeping. Penny did come down to earth enough to make two mugs of tea. I sipped mine while she still chattered on.

'And to think, when I came in from work, I was actually quite thrilled over the news I had waiting for you! I thought you were getting the blues here alone all day, so I fixed you up an interview tomorrow for a rather special nursing post we had in at the bureau. Not that you want to hear about that now!'

I raised my head with interest. Often over the past months I had felt some strange instinctive call back to my old vocation. Ridiculous, because clearly any such work was barred to me. I could imagine the reactions of any self-respecting ward sister when assigned a nurse who'd not only forgotten the hospital where she trained, but wasn't too sure of her own name while training there!

Penny, busy each day with her typewriter and telephone at the Seekers and Finders Employment Bureau, knew that perfectly well.

'What sort of nursing job could I do? I'd be as much use as — '

'As a cracked thermometer? Ah, well, but this is different!'

I had to know why it was different. I pressed until she told me.

'It's not actually nursing,' she explained. 'They need a resident assistant for the summer at The Haven, some sort of experimental clinic in the west country which helps disabled children. The card said, 'Nursing experience useful, sympathy and common sense essential'.'

'I rang up the head bloke and told him about the accident, how ill you were — and about Jeremy, too, all your problems! Well, he asked to see you tomorrow. I thought even just going to the interview might help, Paula, if you were in a rut. That was before I knew you were getting engaged to a perfectly gorgeous man, of course.'

Her attention already was drifting back from the triviality of a temporary summer job to the more important thrill of Hugh's proposal.

I said I was sleepy then and we retired to the big front room we shared with two matching divans, two unmatching wardrobes, and far too much other furniture which had come from the home that had been mine and Robert's.

The rest had been disposed of, but these remaining items I felt must have been part of me and part of him. A desk full of medical textbooks, boxes of classical LPs, drawers of photos, and letters. Not even Penny knew how often I sifted through them, and struggled and ached to remember.

Thankfully, after all her excitement she fell asleep quickly. But, for me, that night brought no rest. I thought about Hugh, the words he had said in the restaurant, the way he had smiled — and the caress of his lips on mine, so gentle, so empty. It was my fault, it wasn't his! My fault that I was striving all the time to recapture the voice and touch of another man . . .

Suddenly, a decision formed in my churning mind. I would go to that interview tomorrow. Not that I stood much chance of being chosen. But the remote chance of escaping for a spell into another world where I could be useful and independent — and able to take a long detached look at my tangled future — was irresistible.

I'll try, I thought, as the dawn glimmered on my framed photograph of Robert watching me from the dressing-table. I have nothing to lose by trying!

★　★　★

'Are you quite sure you know what you're doing?' Penny fretted. 'Honestly, I can't understand — I can't imagine what Hugh will think about it.'

'It's just something I have to do,' I said, trying to convince her.

Luckily, she had no time to argue. Already she had reluctantly produced a Bureau card announcing, *This is to introduce Mrs P. L. Hastings.*

At the door I waved to her as she fled on clattering high heels.

Then I had to concentrate on Jeremy,

who, as usual, pushed his cereal plate away and complained that his Aunt Penny allowed chocolate cake or ice-cream at any hour, nor did she veto the breakfast-time television. During my long illness I couldn't blame Penny for trying to brighten his bereaved, bewildered world by any means, but her little ways and customs were now hard to break.

I was ashamed, at twenty minutes to nine, of the moody-faced and still untidy child — he spiked up his hair as soon as I brushed it down, not to mention the toothpaste on his tie — I produced when Linda Morris from upstairs appeared to make 'the school run.'

We took turns, but in fact she seemed to go more often. Today, as usual, she was bright and cheery, her blonde hair pinned up attractively as she shepherded her seven-year-old, Adam, plus baby Karen in a buggy, plus a puppy on a leash.

Just momentarily, my heart seemed

to plummet, contrasting my struggles this morning with all her brisk proficiency. Wilting on the doorstep in my dressing-gown, the very idea of today's plans seemed now quite ridiculous. But I managed to say, 'Could you collect them this afternoon — and maybe keep Jeremy a while if I'm not back? I have to see someone in London . . . '

'Of course, Paula, no problem!' she assured me. What really hurt was Jeremy's obvious delight at the arrangement as he ducked away from my parting kiss.

Left alone, I had a long, reviving bath, washed my hair, and surveyed it critically in the mirror; still short, it had at least grown back thick and copper-bright after the drastic things done to it in the hospital.

My face was still too pale, too thin, but the scarring on my forehead had almost cleared. I was lucky to be alive, to be standing here prettying myself up! Caroline White hadn't been so lucky.

Presently, a noisy, claustrophobic, tube train decanted me at Victoria. Faced by a confusion of traffic and tall buildings, I queued in cowardly fashion for a taxi.

'Here you are,' the laconic driver announced all too soon, nosing among an array of parked cars to an imposing hotel entrance. With Hugh beside me, with Hugh's hand on my arm, I would have sailed into the foyer undismayed.

But I managed. At the inquiry desk, I asked directions. Soon I was perched on one of the chairs along a carpeted landing, awaiting my turn to enter a certain closed door.

I sat clutching my bag — which held my nursing certificates — which I had no right at all to trade on today, since they really belonged to another person altogether.

After perhaps 20 unnerving minutes, the door opened. Another applicant emerged, an assured and competent-looking girl. She gave me the superior smile of one who already had the job sewn up, and requested, 'Will you go straight in?'

I was on the point of simply running away. Even about that I couldn't make up my mind, whether just to vanish, or more correctly, apologise first, then vanish. Before I decided, a man's voice called from behind the still open door. 'Mrs Hastings? Are you coming in?'

I went in. I mumbled, 'I'm sorry, it'll be a complete waste of time — '

'Let's see, shall we? Hi! My name's Lowell Moroni, I'm the guy you're here to see. Just sit down, we'll have some coffee and talk about it!'

Scarcely helped by this most informal of greetings, I stood still, just looking. Not tall, but powerfully thickset, this man had short-cropped, black curly hair, keen dark eyes in a square, strong face. Probably in his mid 30s, I guessed.

The main reason I stood there rudely staring was because he was confronting me from a sophisticated, power-controlled wheelchair. He glided its chrome frame deftly across the room to telephone for coffee, then back to the table. He waved me to an empty chair opposite.

Hastily, I sat down, abashed by my lapse of manners. But he appeared not to notice it, referring to a file of papers in front of him.

'Paula Hastings. Ah, the lady with all the problems — ' His voice trailed off. Those dark, probing eyes, studied me across the table. 'We've met before!'

'We have?' I said blankly.

'I never forget a face.' He drummed his fingers on the table-top. 'Of course, the South London Children's Hospital. I was there observing and getting in everyone's way. There was that interesting spinal case, the little Indian girl called Rashida who fell out of a second-floor window. You were on the same ward, we had a couple of long chats about Rashida.'

Slowly creeping over me was that chill of horror and unreality always so very frightening when a fragment of the lost past flew up and struck me without warning. Just before the fatal Cornish holiday I had been working at that hospital — I knew that because people had told me; yet I had no memory of the place, nor of the colleagues I'd worked with. There was not even the dimmest picture of Rashida.

Today, after last night's emotional interlude with Hugh and the following hours of sleepless worry, this familiar nightmare was too much. Tears of shock and despair began welling in my eyes. Desperate now just to escape, somehow I was out of my chair, turning blindly towards the door.

But I didn't reach it. A detaining hand held my arm fast.

'Let me go! It's all just a blank, I — I don't remember you!' I choked and struggled vainly to get free. 'I don't remember anything!'

'Sure you don't remember. It's all right, no need to get yourself upset. Just sit down quietly. How long does this damn hotel take to make a pot of coffee?'

'Please, I'd rather just go home!'

'After the tremendous effort it took to come along here? It did, didn't it?'

'Well, yes.' I wondered how he knew, suddenly startled and soothed by the depth of this stranger's understanding. I met, too, a smile that lit up his face. 'I nearly didn't come — and when I got here, I very nearly ran away.'

'I know. But you didn't run away. So we'll take our time and talk about it.'

This time, I gave up arguing. You didn't, it seemed, argue with Lowell Moroni.

The coffee, when it came, was hot and reviving. The room was quiet, street sounds from outside muted and far-off. I sat and suddenly talked and talked, words breaking loose in a great flood.

Without ever meaning to, I found myself recounting almost the whole story of my life: the old fulfilled and efficient Paula, and now the pale imitation Paula who had emerged from long medical care following the accident — struggling vainly to remember, to recapture the image of the man I once loved, to break down the barrier dividing me from my little son. When the words finally petered out, I felt drained.

'Uh-huh. Quite a tale. Thanks for telling me.' His strong hands were piling up the papers on the table, as though with the urgent need to be doing something. 'You want some advice? It'll come back in its own time. You can try to hurry it for the boy's sake — but you can't force it.

'You've done very well already, Mrs Hastings, you know that? All right, you're upset because your life hasn't all fallen back into place — but you're coping, you came along here today — you've picked yourself up enough to think of doing some useful work, and that takes a lot of effort, I know how much!'

Yes, he would know, I thought. Who better than this man who was working under so great a handicap?

'I think maybe this will interest you,' he added, handing over a slim illustrated brochure.

Headed 'The Haven,' it displayed photographs of a large stone-built house with a big glass conservatory at one end and a tower sprouting at the other topped by a turret that must be some sort of observatory. There was charm in the haphazard mellowed walls — and in the spacious sweep of grounds where children and nursing staff were grouped on broad sunny lawns.

Then I turned the page. I saw what the turret had been built to observe: a majestic coastline, towering cliffs, and a rolling white-tipped tide.

'Oh no!' My reaction was one of horror. 'Not if it's by the sea!'

Again I had jumped up, dropping the leaflet on the table. This time Dr Moroni asked with quite comical resignation, 'Are you training to be a jack-in-the-box?'

'I'm sorry, but — it's just no use!'

'Because of the sea? Why not?'

That was a stupid question and all at once a new resentment dawned and began to grow. I wasn't just an interesting case-history of amnesia! I had feelings, I had known grievous hurt.

'Didn't I just tell you, my husband was drowned in the sea?' I demanded shakily.

'Yes. I'm truly sorry about that. But suppose it had been a fatal street accident, would you never walk down a street again?'

'Well, it wasn't a street accident! And I don't have to live by the sea if I don't want to! And,' I flared at him, 'I don't have to answer any more questions!'

He gave another 'Uh-huh,' that most meaningless and infuriating response. 'Will you tell me just one thing more?'

'Well, what is it?' I asked defensively.

He asked with deceptive quiet, 'Have you thought of seeing a psychiatrist?'

'Yes, I have. I saw one a few times

— but I stopped going, he wasn't doing me any good. Look, I'm not crazy, for goodness' sake, I just don't remember!' I fairly blazed this time.

'Did I say you were crazy?' I realised he was smiling at me now with disarming sweetness. Almost, I thought, in satisfaction at achieving this eruption. 'All right, now it's your turn for questions. Ask me anything you want to know about the clinic. If you don't like the location, at least you might be interested in my methods.'

'Of course I'm interested in the children,' I had to agree. I could do little else but pick up the pamphlet again. As I studied the photographs of groups of children digging gardens, cooking meals, painting or singing or whatever, a vigorous verbal commentary began pouring out to me in the doctor's individual way.

His young resident patients were all victims of accident or illness. All had largely overcome, in a physical sense, the havoc caused to them. But none had yet come to terms with their varying disabilities sufficiently to resume their places in families, schools, the normal everyday round of life.

Either from fear of trying again after a traumatic failure, of being ridiculed or pitied, or quite simply a deep-seated horror at being 'different', each child dwelled in its own isolated world — and that in turn could lead to all sorts of behaviour problems.

Kindness alone, the love of parents and friends, often made matters worse. Each time a yearning mother insisted, 'Let me do it for you, darling!' the hope of a complete cure faded a little farther away.

'They've got to understand the impossible is possible, it just takes longer! They've got to stand on their own feet — even if they've no feet to stand on!' The vehement words paused as he interpreted, in uncanny fashion, my sudden glance across the table. 'Yes, me, too! I'm sure you're wondering. Rashida fell through a window — with me it was a flight of stairs. A whole lot of stairs!'

'I see,' I muttered awkwardly. 'Well, at least you're setting your patients a wonderful example, still doing all the work you do.'

He shrugged away the sincerely-meant compliment briskly. 'Not till I get out of this chair for good I'm not!'

I didn't know how to answer that. I turned him back to the less personal aspects of The Haven, the treatment he gave the children, his success rate with them so far.

That brought me another tide of explanations. He had failed, he admitted frankly, with a first attempt to start his therapeutic community back home. 'Chiefly, the staff walked out — then the money was all spent!' he told me with more of that startling candour.

But now he was beginning anew. His aim was that after a few months of his special regime of rehabilitation, the children could return to an outside world they had now been taught to face.

As yet, The Haven had run only a few weeks at half capacity, so he had no real proof that his methods worked. But he was quite sure he would soon convince all the unbelievers who labelled him a crank with a big mouth!

His sureness, the fierce and unsparing driving force behind it, came across to me. It was hard not to believe him.

In the vital search for suitable staff, he was rattling on, who could understand the patients' problems more completely than I could? Never mind worrying about my blanked-out past, it was the present, the future, that mattered most!

'How about some positive thinking? I've made up my mind about you, Mrs — oh, it's Paula, isn't it? I can see you've a whole lot to give. And giving it would help you, I'm sure of it. OK, you do have troubles, but I'll take a chance on them. I'll start you on a trial basis — part-time if you want, we don't want

to overtax your strength — accommo-
dation for you and your little boy
provided, of course. So, come on, how
soon can you start?'

I thought quite desperately, this was
too fast, far too fast! I stammered.
'Well, thank you for the offer, but . . . '
Then came inspiration. 'But I can't
really decide till I've talked to Hugh
Egerton. You see, last night he — asked
me to marry him! Oh, he's been
wonderful to me and to Jeremy since
the accident — and he saved our lives,
of course. He's quite well known,
perhaps you've seen his TV show?'

'I've seen him.' Abruptly, he began
bundling his papers together. 'If you'd
said at the start you were all set for a
career as Mrs Megastar Egerton, I'd
have agreed with you we were wasting
our time sitting here kicking your job
prospects around. Nice meeting you.
Mrs Hastings.'

It wasn't so much his words as the
offensive way he said them that made
my blood boil a second time. Did I look

like a parasite or a gold digger? What right had he to assume I would inevitably opt for ease and glamour above any passing interest in becoming a humble care assistant to his group of troubled children?

'There's no need to disparage Hugh! He may be a megastar, but he does marvellous work. I'm not really surprised your staff walked out, Dr Moroni — and I'm not sure I could stand working for you very long, either. But, as I haven't settled anything yet with Hugh, I might agree to take the job to help out for a few weeks — just to see if I can do it!'

'Good.' He smiled at me disarmingly. 'I knew you would.'

I was still in such a fever of irritation that I had quite forgotten the doubts and fears that had haunted me only an hour ago.

The brief remainder of the interview, just mundane details, swept over my head. I was to check with my doctor at home, post on references, study the notes he handed over. I would ring about a date when I could travel down to The Haven.

★   ★   ★

Outside, spring sunshine glimmered. The street was still as busy, traffic churning past. The cool, fresh air met me like a sudden awakening blast of reality.

But this past hour, too, had been real, and later, I would need to explain it to Hugh. The thought of his kindness and care possessed me suddenly. There was no escaping the truth, that, after all he said to me last night, I had immediately gone off after an independent job miles away!

All at once I was very tired, and my head was beginning to ache badly. A bus for the station was just leaving from a stop a few yards away, and I moved slowly on to join the people still waiting there. Nearby was a paper-seller in a doorway, and mechanically I groped for some change. Somehow, I must divert my thoughts on this homeward journey.

In the bus queue, I stuffed Dr Moroni's notes farther down in my bag and my mind.

A moment later, I was standing on the pavement rigid with shock, the newspaper shaking in my hands as I stared at a photograph of Hugh and myself; a picture taken after the accident when I was well enough to pose with him. There I was, in long dressing-gown and a filmy scarf around my head and there was Hugh by my chair, his protective hand on my arm.

Yet it wasn't the photo that so transfixed me, but its caption 'Wedding Bells!' — and a paragraph by the 'Daily Chat' columnist, who I knew was a friend of Hugh's.

Yes, delighted to confirm the whisper that they'll soon be ringing for 'The Friendship Man' Hugh Egerton and the girl he so bravely saved in the tragic accident when his boat Sea Queen was lost off the coast of Cornwall.

Attractive titian-haired Paula Hastings is still suffering serious effects from her ordeal so the couple plan a quiet Alpine honeymoon and afterwards a peaceful country home where she can continue to rest and recuperate.

Last night, did I really say 'Yes' to Hugh? Did we settle those detailed plans? At this moment I didn't know, I couldn't think, and yet here it all was before me in black and white!

Eerily, the street sounds were changing around me. The rush of traffic was surging water, engulfing and choking. The buildings were tall cliffs where waves boiled and thundered. I was sinking, struggling, the breath bubbling in my throat . . .

'Hold on to her! Someone call an ambulance!'

'You'll be all right, dear,' a stout, kindly woman was saying.

'Don't crowd round, let her breathe! I'm a doctor, I know the young lady

— can you bring her into the hotel?' At last, a voice I knew, the sort of voice to take instant command. I wasn't sure how I reached the hotel lobby, then water was being held to my lips. I became aware of dark eyes looking into mine.

'I — I almost remembered,' I heard myself trying to whisper. 'We were in the water, then — oh, dear God, he wasn't there any more . . . '

'Was it Robert? You remembered Robert? Try to tell me, Paula.'

'Yes. No. I don't know!' Unconsciously, I was clinging fast to a hand that held mine warmly and strongly. I needed that human contact.

'You've had a shock, just take it easy. Has this happened to you before?'

'Not really, just tiny flashbacks — I've told Hugh about them — but not like this. Oh, I'm sorry for making such a scene.'

'Don't worry, I'm glad I was looking out of the window. When you feel better, I'll get you a cab home. Shall I ring your sister to come here?'

'Thank you,' I said inadequately. 'No, don't worry Penny. I really am sorry to be a nuisance, Dr — er . . . when I know you're so busy . . . '

'Moroni,' he prompted. 'Lowell Giullio Moroni. Why not make it just Lowell?'

I hadn't thought, during our turbulent interview upstairs, that he could be so gentle and so kind. Rather wistfully now, I mumbled, 'Well, at least it has ended all the uncertainty about the job. You certainly won't want me now, will you?'

'I'm not so sure. Maybe you could do things for The Haven, and The Haven could do things for you.' I wasn't sure what he meant, but he made it plainer. 'I'd like to try to help you, if you'll come and help with the kids. So — is it a deal?'

At this moment I didn't think of being sick and bewildered, or of Hugh, or Penny, or Jeremy, or really anything at all. I was just aware of a strange sense of relief.

I said quite simply, 'Yes, please. Yes, it's a deal.'

I needed a haven. Now I had one.

2

'Kev, you're wonderful!' Penny hugged him vigorously, leather jacket, orange crash helmet, curly beard and all, as he returned from a meteoric dash to the nearby Chinese take-away. 'Now, be an angel and help me dish it out. No, not you, Paula, love, it's your party, so you sit still and look pretty!'

As far as my sister was concerned, any excuse for a party was a good one. But I suspected this particular party, on the eve of my departure, had deep, dark motives. Only a small gathering, it was supposed to celebrate 'Nurse Hastings getting back in action.' More likely, I thought, Penny hoped it would per-suade me I just couldn't tear myself away tomorrow from everyone I knew.

All this past week, it had been hard to stick to my decision to join the staff of The Haven. The conversations with

Hugh — mainly by telephone, as he was away on a series of engagements, had been uncomfortable. He never raised his voice in anger or reproach. But I knew he was startled and hurt.

'If you want a change of scene,' he kept insisting across the miles, 'you know you only have to say so. Didn't we agree I'd look after you? Why not let me fix up a quiet holiday for you somewhere in the sun?'

I tried to say that a holiday soaking up sunshine wasn't at all what I needed. That would offer no challenge, answer no questions — indeed, only provide more chance to brood on the blanked-out part of my life that so haunted me.

But this job at The Haven, at once so tempting and so frightening, would prove whether I could still function usefully. I could perhaps achieve independence, rely again on my own judgment, and believe again in my own identity. I think it was too much to expect Hugh to understand all that.

Quite apart from Hugh, there were

other problems. There was Jeremy, who reacted violently to the idea of moving to the seaside and meeting lots of new friends. Adam upstairs was his friend, he wailed, and he didn't want to leave Adam, nor their mutual school — which previously he had called 'horrible.' Nothing I could say would penetrate his fixed state of sulks.

Last but not least, there was Penny, blaming herself totally for my differences with Hugh and for all this upheaval. 'Why didn't I just keep my big stupid mouth shut about that job?' she'd said. That was why I couldn't refuse her idea of this party, why I was sitting here tonight in a new dress, longing to escape, but trying hard to be sociable.

'So when do you expect your wedding to be, Paula, dear?' an elderly neighbour of ours was asking with rapt interest. She was one of the two Miss Coombes, who fed all the stray cats in the district, and had sent me in strange milk-puddings and stranger brews of herbal tea during my convalescence. 'When we saw that piece in the paper we were so thrilled! Weren't we, Louisa?'

I tried not to sigh, and patiently repeated to them the set excuses I had given everyone else agog for wedding news — including the local Press who'd turned up on my doorstep with a photographer at the ready. Hugh had a full work schedule, I said, I had work commitments, too, for a few weeks, and after that everyone must just wait and see.

Privately, Hugh had produced a feasible enough explanation for the shattering newspaper item. He had merely chatted to the friend who wrote the column, and either he'd been too vague or she'd misunderstood, and she'd jumped the gun. It would soon be forgotten. At least, Hugh said it would be.

I still hadn't told him whether or not I would marry him. Quite simply, I still just didn't know —

'Well, mind you give us plenty of warning, we wouldn't miss it,' Linda from upstairs assured me. 'Good grief, don't you realise you'll be the envy of every female aged eight to eighty? In a few years, Paula, just remember us poor mortals when you're supervising your nannies and chauffeurs and gardeners.'

'Hugh doesn't have a chauffeur — but perhaps he should, he's taking so long to arrive here tonight,' Penny grumbled. 'He was opening some special park today somewhere.'

'A scented garden for the blind,' I supplied absently.

'Bless him, what a lovely idea,' the two Miss Coombes breathed in awed unison.

Penny was more concerned about her waiting refreshments, and finally announced we would have to begin.

I went on sitting there, watching Jeremy and Adam wading through crisps and peanuts in front of the television, hoping no one could see my mounting anxiety while I waited for

Hugh. It was almost an hour later, with the party just petering out, that he arrived.

Penny proudly ushered him in saying, 'Hugh, seven o'clock I said, and seven o'clock I meant!'

That so familiar, so appealing voice, apologised gently. 'I ran into a big tailback. I just had to sit there imagining you cursing me.'

'Well, never mind, I won't curse you any more now you're here. Come on, let me introduce you to everyone!'

As I met his eyes across the room, he smiled at me. It didn't help much. I knew that when this ordeal of a party ended, between the two of us I faced an ordeal still greater.

Penny wasn't disappointed by the awed and delighted reactions to Hugh Egerton's arrival. He chatted and smiled, and was his usual self, which meant he could quietly charm everyone there.

Quite soon the party broke up, because the old ladies had to feed their cats, and the children be bundled off to bed. Kevin's home-bound motorbike shattered the peace of the night. Linda's family melted away upstairs.

'Why do I have to go to bed early when I don't have school tomorrow?' Jeremy grumbled as Penny whisked him off to the back regions. He didn't even answer when I promised to come and say good night.

I sighed involuntarily.

Hugh said, 'So he's not very happy about your plans, either. That makes two of us. Three, counting Penny.'

'I know,' I muttered. This was the dreaded moment.

He sat close beside me on the settee and held my hand.

'Hugh, I'm sorry if you're angry, but I've made up my mind. It's not just that I have to know if I can do this. But I've been thinking, I'm sure it — it's what Robert would want me to do . . . '

This time it was Hugh who sighed. 'There's no possible way you can know that. Haven't you been told before that

49

this constant obsession of yours with the past isn't just unhealthy, it could even be dangerous? Oh, of course you've been through a terrible time, you need to start afresh. But not this way,' he went on relentlessly.

'You're talking about haring off at a moment's notice to the very part of the country you should avoid — uprooting Jeremy when he's had troubles enough — and most of all, trying to take on responsibilities you're not nearly well enough to cope with. I can't imagine any sensible person employing you, let alone a man who calls himself a doctor.'

The velvet voice wasn't smooth. It now had quite an edge to it.

'He knows all about my health,' I protested. 'He said he'd make allowances, and I'm sure he's an extremely good doctor and a very dedicated man.'

'You may be in for a disillusionment,' Hugh said deliberately. 'You know in my work I meet with all sorts of good causes — mostly genuine, a few not so genuine — and the name Moroni rang a bell with me. I've made some inquiries, and I'm afraid that over in the States, The Haven he ran folded up suddenly. I haven't the full details yet, but there were — shall we say, suspicious circumstances?'

'I know it all went wrong,' I broke in wearily. 'He told me, he didn't pretend otherwise. He said mainly he had staff troubles.'

'I think there was more to it than that. A lot more.'

'All right, that still doesn't affect the work he's doing now, does it? I just don't want to hear any secondhand scandals about him, thank you. I shall see for myself and make up my own mind.' I heard my own voice rise, quite shrill with anger and strain, but I felt that Hugh was being underhand in the way he was trying to persuade me to reconsider tomorrow's departure.

Of course, I couldn't really explain how all these past days I had been clinging to the memory of Lowell Moroni's words — 'I'll help you if you'll help me' — as though it were an anchor in a vast ocean of doubt. There was no logical explanation for that.

If, by now, my own face was passionately ablaze, I realised Hugh's was quite startlingly pale and stern.

'Very well. If you won't listen to reason there's no more to be said. But don't think I'm giving up, Paula. Perhaps in the end you'll have to pay attention to me.'

He was barely managing to crush down hurt and frustration and deep, deep anger. I was just a little frightened. I had never seen him like this before.

It was a vast relief when Penny came bouncing back. Hugh quickly regained his usual humour, but he soon stood up and fumbled for his car keys.

'But you've scarcely got here,' Penny protested.

'I know. Sorry. But Paula will have a tiring day tomorrow. Which reminds me — I'm not happy about the hassle of this long rail journey. Can't I send a car along instead? Door to door service?'

'Sounds marvellous!' Penny agreed for me while I was still hesitating and mumbling that people must stop wrapping me in cotton-wool. It sounded very ungracious.

'All right, I'll get something fixed up,' Hugh said, either not hearing me or choosing not to hear. 'I know we'll all feel much happier about you, Paula, knowing you'll arrive safely.'

This was the Hugh I knew, gentle, kind, and caring. I felt suddenly guilty about that horrible scene a few moments ago. Perhaps it had been all my fault. Perhaps, indeed, I had treated him badly.

All at once I didn't want him to leave. I overheard him reassuring Penny quietly in the hall, 'Don't worry, we'll both keep in close touch and as soon as she finds it too much, I'll bring her home. I'd give it a couple of weeks, no more — ' After that, he came back into the room to say goodbye to me. His arms held me warm and close.

'Please try to understand. I do

appreciate you're trying to prove you can stand on your own feet and do something worthwhile in the world. But there's just no need. And — I shall miss you very much.'

'Will you?' I whispered foolishly. I wished I could believe it enough to throw my arms around him and do as he'd suggested. But I couldn't do that. In some strange way, only my mind believed. My heart didn't quite believe.

With sudden tears in my eyes, I clung to him momentarily as though I couldn't let him go. In that instant I was very near giving in. But I didn't and the moment passed. His car swept off into the darkness.

* * *

The morning was sunny and beautiful. Well before seven I was up and about bringing Penny an offering of tea.

She had arranged to go in late to work, intending to escort Jeremy and myself to the train. Now, it was just a matter of killing time till the car appeared, and checking that everything was packed.

When our transport did arrive, it lifted Jeremy's spirits at once. Large and opulent, it was driven by a breezy young man who saluted us with a cheery 'Morning!'

While the mound of luggage was being swallowed up in the boot, Jeremy was already out on the pavement, jigging up and down in approval.

'Cor, this is great! I bet we'll do two hundred on the motorway!'

I hoped sedately that we wouldn't. In the doorway, Penny kissed me. She kept saying, 'I'll see you again, soon, Paula love.'

'Of course, Kev must bring you down for a week-end,' I agreed, purposely misunderstanding. 'And thank you for all you've done. I can't ever thank you enough — '

She pooh-poohed that, her blue eyes moist.

As I slid into the back seat beside

Jeremy, I carried away that last picture of her, bravely smiling, waving like an erratic windmill. Then she was left behind, she and her world, the tall old house made bright with her ready laughter and her loving warmth. She had helped me build a new life when my life seemed over. Now, there lay ahead another new world, suddenly chilling, peopled only by strangers.

The sun stayed bright when the metropolis was left far behind us. It was still shining later when we stopped for a coffee-break, and again presently for a leisurely lunch. I nibbled a sandwich and steered Jeremy away from some lurid desserts.

By now the novelty of the journey had worn off. He didn't want to trace our progress on maps, or look at comics. He kept clamouring to sit in the front of the car, and wondering dismally what Adam was doing.

Eventually, the drowsy warmth and the motion of the car, on top of yesterday's late night, actually lulled him to sleep. After that, we stuck fast in a hold-up caused by some accident. Despite my anxiety about the job ahead, I began dozing myself.

I dreamed about Hugh, about Penny, and about The Haven. The next thing I knew the driver's voice was announcing, 'We're here, Mrs Hastings.'

The car was just turning off a narrow lane into a tall gateway. A nameplate proclaimed *The Haven, Residential Clinic* — and another notice said, *Please keep this gate SHUT, this means YOU! L. Moroni, Doctor in Charge*.

Roused from my unexpected slumbers, I blinked around in disbelief. But there was no doubt the journey was over. I saw green lawns, a walled garden bright with wallflowers and irises, an enclosed playground with swings and slides. Beyond, I could see a tennis court and games field, and some sort of miniature farm. Everything was dominated by the stone-built bulk of a big rambling house, crowned by an unmistakable castellated tower.

In the early dusk of this beautiful evening, through which glowed the delicate mauve and pure white of blossom-heavy lilacs, it all looked mellow and drowsy. But lights at the windows, parked cars, and a dusty yellow mini-bus, showed that the place was very much alive and tenanted.

I gave a crumpled, bleary-eyed Jeremy a quick shake and emerged stiffly from the car, trying to smooth down my skirt. Really, I had never felt less like facing a new beginning.

'Mrs Hastings? I was expecting you a couple of hours ago.' A decidedly daunting reception committee of one awaited me in what seemed to be the main entrance. Large of stature, grim of face, her navy nylon overall straining at its seams, she had steel-grey hair and sharp, pale-hued eyes which were surveying me and my travel-worn state unsmilingly. 'Well, you'd better come in. Is all this luggage yours?'

Her manner made me feel I had

transported everything bar the kitchen sink. I was quite sorry when the friendly driver wished me 'Good luck!' and beat a quick retreat.

Inescapably, the spacious hallway of The Haven yawned before me. I held Jeremy's hand and looked around. On either side were primrose-painted doors, with a broad staircase leading upwards — and also, I noticed, a lift. As well as a big notice-board and rows of child-size coats on hooks, a great many paintings adorned the walls, obviously the work of the children.

A shelf displayed several somewhat cock-eyed models of ships and cars. Cactus plants, their pots lettered 'Angela' and 'Geoff' and 'Liz,' paraded on a window-ledge. Last, but not least, several fish swam languidly in a tank, and a cat and three kittens reposed in an old soap-carton.

Even Hugh would have had to admit that the general impression was bright and interesting, far more like the home of a big busy family than any sort of hospital or clinic. Already I could see that the old building had been most attractively and thoughtfully adapted. Someone — and I had a good idea who it was — had worked very hard on The Haven.

My dismay of a moment ago was already fading, helped on its way by strains of music drifting from some-where, an accompanying piano and tuneful, upraised young voices. Jeremy, who loathed music, was visibly squirm-ing.

'That sounds nice,' I ventured to comment.

'You think so? Wait till you've heard it several hundred times.' The formidable lady in navy nylon had just spotted some muddy footmarks along the hall. I was glad they weren't mine. 'I'm Mrs Burns,' she informed me tartly. I wondered if she was some sort of housekeeper.

'How do you do?' I said politely. 'I expect you know I'm a new helper here.'

'Have you worked at a place like this before?'

'Not exactly. I used to be a nurse.'

She said, 'Oh!' as though that should have endowed me with more sense. 'Well, you'll find it needs getting used to. I've been here since the place opened. Gave my notice after the first week, I'm just waiting till they get a replacement. Well,' she added more tartly still. 'I'll tell Dr Moroni you're here as soon as he's free — it's more than anyone's life is worth to interrupt that singing. You'd better come upstairs and I'll show you where I've put you. Not The Ritz, you understand, just attics.'

I assured her that the attics would do very well.

We went part of the way in the lift with the luggage. The steep, narrow top stairway had to be ascended on foot. Breathing hard from the climb, she pushed open another of the primrose doors.

'This is yours. Nurse Farmer had it

till she walked out. I've put in another bed for the little boy.'

I was itching to know why Nurse Farmer had walked out, but couldn't quite manage to ask. Instead, I surveyed my new home. The big, strangely-shaped attic, its walls and sloping ceilings papered in a pastel patchwork design, had been split into two parts, scrupulously clean, and simply furnished. Both had a bed, and the larger also a table and chairs. The window overlooked a sweep of spectacular coastline. I turned away from that in haste.

'Behind here,' Mrs Burns was going on, pointing out a small screened-off kitchen area, 'you can make tea and toast and so on so long as you don't set the place on fire — someone will one of these days. Your bathroom's next door. Shared, of course.'

'Thank you, it's all very nice.'

'So long as you think so. I never could abide attics. Freeze you to death in the winter, fry you in your bed in the summer.' She turned to the door, then looked back grudgingly. 'You've missed our six-thirty meal. I suppose you'd better both come down to the dining-room when you're ready, I'll find you something.'

Maybe she did have a kind heart, well hidden away. I was willing to give her the benefit of the doubt. But Jeremy evidently wasn't, for she was scarcely out of earshot before his stunned silence ended.

'She's horrible! Worse than that grumpy dinner-lady at school! And we can't live here in this dump, we haven't even got a TV!'

'We can get ourselves one,' I said patiently. 'We've only just arrived, so let's give it all a chance. Come on, choose where you want to sleep.'

'I don't care. I'm not sleeping here! I want to go back to Aunt Penny's!'

It was hard to be angry with Jeremy, who looked so very tired and miserable. After a moment I gave up trying to jolly him along. As usual, I simply didn't know how to reach him.

Maybe if I took him downstairs for some supper, then bundled him firmly off to bed, he would be more amenable in the morning. Maybe.

★　★　★

Below, the choir practice evidently was just over. The singers were filtering through from wherever they sang. In the big hallway it was startling for me, let alone for Jeremy, to encounter more or less en masse The Haven's dozen or so young patients.

The door of a big pleasant lounge stood open now, disclosing colourful groups of chairs and tables and cushioned sofas — and a large television, which I nudged Jeremy to point out, but he seemed too overwhelmed to notice. The room was far less absorbing than the chattering group of under-elevens — whose voices suddenly were silenced by a first glimpse of strangers in their midst.

A wave of deepest concern came to me as I looked around. Several of the children had physical handicaps or the scars of serious injury. Two or three had difficulty in walking, one peered through thick lenses of spectacles. There were others whose problems weren't so apparent. Only the varying degrees of fear or dismay or even anger in their faces were common to all.

'Hello, everyone,' I said in the friendliest way I could. 'I was just admiring your singing. It sounded wonderful.'

No one answered. Some stared back at me, stonily or suspiciously. Some retreated in alarmed haste. Unhappily I struggled to find the right words, but none came. Only, far down in my mind, something mistily stirred — as though it were a ghost of recollection from far-off days when once Nurse Hastings had coped with happy efficiency in a long forgotten hospital ward. But the image flickered and died, eluding capture.

A new voice behind me ended the awkward silence. 'You must be Mrs Hastings? And no one's looking after you, that's too bad! I'm Faye Prescott, how do you do? Hello, Jeremy, you're a big boy, aren't you?'

Jeremy, who wasn't a big boy and knew he wasn't, glowered at her. The words did have a condescending ring. But I welcomed her intervention, gladly returning her bright smile. She was, I guessed, about 30. Tall, slim, and ash blonde, she had classically straight features, clear eyes more green than grey. She wore a dark pencil skirt and a cream silk shirt with a certain assured and stylish ease that needed no enhancing frills.

'Have you been shown round yet and met everyone? No? Then can I help?' she offered. 'Oh, does Lowell know you're here?'

'I don't think so.' I was a little startled at that familiar use of his first name. 'I've only seen Mrs Burns so far. Is she the housekeeper?'

'Loosely speaking! She has her finger in lots of pies — not just the ones she cooks. I'm the resident teacher here — officially, that is. I help out with practically everything. Everyone here is supposed to do everything.'

She broke off there as two staff members came towards us, coaxing along a dark-haired little girl who had obviously been crying and hadn't yet quite stopped. Miss Prescott hailed them.

'Ah, you're just in time to meet the new arrivals.'

One of the care assistants, Annie Beecher, was plump, greying and motherly. The other, in total contrast, was French, teenaged and chic, who was 'learning ze trade,' she told me with a pert smile and a winning accent. Sophie Dupres had come over originally on a study course in pediatrics. 'And you couldn't learn more about children than from our little bunch, dear,' Mrs Beecher told me earnestly.

After that, I was taken on an

introductory round of the little bunch who had already so aroused my concern. Faye Prescott put names to faces; too many, of course, to digest all at once. By now, despite her ready help, I wasn't altogether sure I wholly liked the elegant Miss Prescott. Not only Jeremy was on the receiving end of her condescending manner.

By now, Jeremy was quite bowled over by everything so new and strange and was trying to merge into my shadow — until one deceptively angelic-looking boy started pulling horrific faces at him behind Faye's back, then he soon began replying in kind. Just as a really lurid contest was developing, everyone's interest in it was brought to an instant end by the approaching sound of a power-driven wheelchair.

I looked round with quick expectancy at my new employer. The few days since our first meeting hadn't at all dimmed my first impression of him yet he seemed now squarer, darker, sterner, his dark vivid eyes even more penetrating. Also, I thought he looked older. Or perhaps tiredness emphasised the deeply-etched lines in his face.

He greeted me with the same 'Hi!' that had amazed me at the interview, and another 'Hi, make yourself at home!' for Jeremy. Then, he turned purposefully to the children.

'All right, gang. Who's on hamster duty this week — Eddie, Camilla? The cage is disgusting, either clean it out right now or give the poor little guys some boots to wear! Who left the gardening things lying around? Julie and Angie? OK, you get them put away — and whoever spilled milk all over the kitchen, I'd go and see Mrs Burns before she comes to see you!'

Magically, peace and emptiness descended on the room as everyone scattered, their leisure short lived. Of course, discipline was important, rules must be kept, but the thought came to me that maybe most of that sad little group might do better with a warm drink and a warm cuddle before bed.

Just a little chilled, I felt, too, that my own treatment was somewhat offhand. 'Be in my office in half an hour, OK?' he ordered me briefly as he glided past.

Since the day in London that had brought us strangely close, we had spoken just once by telephone in strictly business-like fashion, yet somehow I had anticipated more warmth in his welcome today.

There seemed no point in lingering any longer, and with supper now forgotten (and heaven help me if Mrs Burns had already laid it out!) I steered Jeremy back upstairs to our own quarters. Thankfully, he was tired enough just to fall into bed in the smaller room and pull the covers over his head to shut out the whole world. I just regretted that he was shutting me out, too.

I sat quietly on my own bed until he was asleep. Then I left him, my light still on and the dividing door ajar. With thoughts and feelings in turmoil, I set off to find Dr Moroni's office.

'In there.' Sophie obligingly indicated a door at the back of the hall.

I tapped on the door, then tentatively pushed it open. The room was empty, large and pleasant, if not over tidy, with abundant plants in pots, shelves of higgledy-piggledy books and files, and a medley of photographs and pictures dotted around the walls where they could best be seen.

Surprisingly dominant was a piano, standing open and scattered with sheet music. I noticed there was no stool by the piano. I noticed, too, an empty wheelchair standing near the big, cluttered desk. But for that desk the room was wholly unlike an office.

The patio doors stood wide open, letting in a cool evening breeze. As I stood there gazing around me, there were sounds on the patio just outside.

'Were you waiting for me? Sorry,' a distinctly breathless voice said. 'My evening constitutional. Rain or shine, I never miss it.'

Just returning from his 'walk' in the dusky grounds, Lowell Moroni negotiated the step up into the room in a brisk fashion — but plainly with difficulty, depending heavily on the crutches he used. Despite the night chill, his broad, dark forehead was beaded with a moisture.

I took an instinctive step forward to help, as he made for the waiting wheelchair. Then, instinctively again, I stopped, offering instead, 'Shall I shut the doors?'

'OK.' Evidently he allowed that. 'Thanks. Sorry about the exhibition. A while ago, a renowned specialist showed me a gallery of X-rays and vowed I'd never move again without wheels under me, let alone walk with the feet God gave me. In a few more years I'll prove the guy a liar.'

Uncertain what to say, I was busy for a moment fastening the doors and pulling the curtains across. I heard a half-stifled gasp. When I looked round, he was back in his chair, very much in command. But for the damp, black hair on his forehead, I almost doubted what I had just seen.

'Now let's talk about you,' he announced briskly. 'So you didn't back out of starting here. How are you feeling?'

'I'm fine. No, I didn't back out. Did you think I would?'

'I thought you might. I hoped you wouldn't. And welcome, in case no one's said it yet. No more dramatic collapses at bus stops?'

'Certainly not! I don't make a practice of them.'

'I believe you.' He made a soothing gesture with those mobile hands I remembered. 'I suppose you didn't tell your family much about it.'

'Well . . . No,' I admitted. Really, he scarcely needed to ask all these questions, with his uncannily probing eyes seeking out their own answers. 'I didn't want to worry my sister, she was upset anyway about my coming here. And so was Hugh. Especially when I had the idea Robert would have wanted me to come . . . '

This time the thought wasn't denounced as ridiculous. He nodded. 'Sure he would! He was a doctor, you were a nurse. A family tradition of healing and caring.'

Momentarily, I was warmed, strangely moved, by a glimpse of his brilliant, unexpected smile.

'I can't promise you an easy life here, but I think you'll soon feel you did the right thing. Is Jeremy safely asleep? Right, first a grand tour of the premises, you form your own impressions and ask all the questions you want — then we'll come back here and have a good, long discussion about the basic routine.'

He was already on his way to the door, waving me to go ahead.

The next half-hour, spent exploring The Haven under his animated guidance, flew past magically. I saw the dining-room, the classroom with desks and blackboards, the modest little gymnasium, the art room, a hobbies room scattered with half-made models, sewing, raffia work, and so on. Then, of course, there were cloakrooms, bedrooms, and a big, modern kitchen.

It was too dark to see outside, where he said flowers and vegetables and fruit were rigorously cultivated and where there were various sports facilities.

Throughout the tour, he seemed to have a bright word for everyone we met, and was answered deferentially. At the end of it all, back in his office, I sat by the big desk which was littered with files and notes.

Now he talked on and on, his face alight and absorbed. The discussion he had promised proved distinctly one-sided.

'One hundred per cent participation therapy,' was the phrase that stuck in my mind. The patients, he kept repeating, took part in everything around them. And that did mean everything. Not just Miss Prescott's school and the usual games and educational outings, but they helped to cook their meals and clean their rooms, they fed and cared for the establishment's pets, they dug the gardens and fetched the shopping.

I did venture to suggest that sometimes it might be simply impossible for one specific inmate to achieve one specific task. But that was quickly squashed.

'We don't allow the word 'can't' at The Haven. Make an excuse for one and you've got to make excuses for all the rest — and you've sabotaged the whole system. All right, sometimes things get rugged. But it's our job to provide the answers, that's why we're here. That's why the kids are here. So if you haven't the patience or the guts for the job, now's the time to say so.'

I said only, 'I see.' I went on quietly listening. Yet, as I kept on remembering that pathetic bunch of children I had seen tonight, I felt a vague unease. The Haven offered wonderful facilities, and not for one moment did I doubt the bright and shining sincerity of this man's intentions. But perhaps his regime, in some cases, might be a little too harsh.

Maybe he did bully and badger his patients into improvement, but surely those forlorn little souls deserved a little less driving, a little more leading along the way he wanted them to go?

I still hadn't found words to express those nagging doubts, without appearing to be trying to teach him his business on my very first day, when we were interrupted by the phone ringing on his desk. For a moment, I was relieved to have time to think.

Only for a moment. He passed the phone a little grimly to me.

Embarrassed, I mumbled, 'For me? I'm sorry — ' Then I forgot all about apologising, as a quiet, gentle voice spoke my name.

'Oh, Hugh, it's so nice to hear from you!'

There were so many things I wanted to say to him. All at once I realised how many — and I realised, too, the distance dividing us, not merely for the duration of one of his work engagements, but for weeks, maybe months, ahead. Of course, that had been part of my plan in coming here to be apart from him, to give me time to think . . .

He was asking about the journey down, just ordinary routine questions. He sounded concerned about me. When he wanted my first impression of The Haven I stuttered and stammered awkwardly, painfully aware this wasn't at all a private conversation. Dr Moroni hadn't left the room, nor had he suggested where else I could take my call. He was just sitting there, waiting for me to finish.

'As soon as I get some free time, I'll be down to see you,' Hugh was promising.

I said that would be nice. I had to say also that I was tied up just now, perhaps we could talk tomorrow.

'Of course. Tomorrow,' he agreed. 'So long as you're quite sure you're all right. I'll tell Penny I've spoken to you. Good night, Paula.'

His voice was soft and sympathetic. I wanted to cling to the sound of it.

Instead, I had to return to the dark, watchful gaze across the desk, and my interrupted briefing session. It was difficult to channel my thoughts back to it. I must, indeed, have sat there with a foolishly, faraway look on my face, because Lowell Moroni began summarily bundling together the files he had spread out.

'OK. I need a 100 per cent concentration from you. So we'll start afresh tomorrow.'

Undoubtedly, this man with his 100 per cent this and 100 per cent that, had a fierce impatience and arrogance about him that was hard to accept in large quantities. I had thought so at our first meeting, and now I thought so again. But, as I got to my feet at the brusque dismissal, he added with that sudden winning smile, 'Go and get a good sleep, you must need it, Paula.'

'Thank you,' I said lamely. Confused, I turned to the door, cager now to escape. But, on my way, I couldn't help staring more closely at a portrait over the piano — a rather portly, very dark and Italian-looking gentleman, gazing intensely into the distance and clutching a sheaf of music. There was something about that face. Quite without meaning to, I remarked, 'That wouldn't be your father?'

'My grandfather.' He whirred round the desk to my side, surveying the picture, too. 'Come on, don't tell me you don't recognise Guilio Moroni? The Guilio Moroni? His 'Cavaradossi' interpretation is still talked about at La Scala.'

The name of the famous opera house at least told me he was talking about a singer. I apologised, 'I'm sorry to be so ignorant. Robert liked opera, I still have his records.'

'G. M. made records — but before the hi-fi era. He's a legend. In the best traditions he ran away as a kid to sing in the streets for a few lire — and was eventually discovered by a wealthy benefactor, and never looked back. He's past eighty now, and still sings like a bird. He lives in Italy with — ' He stopped abruptly, then added, 'With the family.'

With deep interest in this most unexpected and romantic story, I surveyed respectfully the face in the painting. I said gravely, 'There's definitely a likeness.'

'So people say. But he has more chins. I hope!'

'So you sing, too?' I had to ask, remembering in a new light the choir practice earlier.

His answer was quite startling. He lifted his head and launched straight into a very well-known aria, familiar even to me — in a lilting, soaring tenor, a voice of sweetness and power and passion. It seemed in its sheer beauty to speak to my soul. When the melody ended all too soon, there were tears flooding my eyes. I didn't need to understand the words.

'Puccini, of course,' he said. 'The unfortunate hero of 'Tosca' who's waiting to be shot at dawn.'

'It's beautiful. The way you sing it, it's the most beautiful thing I've ever heard . . . ' I wanted to ask him to sing it again. I wondered about the depth of emotion he put into those last words. 'I'm sure your grandfather couldn't ever have surpassed you,' I insisted earnestly. 'Surely you could have been just as famous a singer if — if — '

' 'If' is a word I never mess with,' he said abruptly. The light in his face, the softness in his voice and his eyes vanished.

'Sorry,' I said. I always seemed to be saying that. I retreated to the door with a subdued, 'Good night, Dr — '

'Didn't I tell you before to make it Lowell? How many more times do you need telling?'

Outside, still shattered, I found all seemed deserted after the earlier bustle. But on my way upstairs I was brought suddenly back to reality by the sound of a child's muffled sobs.

It didn't take me long to find a corner of the big lobby wasn't deserted after all. A frail, dark-haired little girl in a pink nightie was crouching under the stand holding the big fish-tank.

I remembered the name I had been told, and the potted history. Bridget Poole, a recent arrival, had been saved from a tragic blaze in which her widowed mother died.

'Bridget, what's wrong, pet?' I kneeled down to get to her level.

'Won't you come out and tell me about it?'

She shook her head violently. 'No! I just want to go back home!'

'I know,' I sympathised. 'I'm new here, too. Why not come out and let's talk about it?'

It took a while before I could discover the cause of her present distress. Today she should have fed the rabbits, but she was afraid of them, so she hadn't done so. Now she was unable to sleep in case they starved.

I offered at once to feed them myself while she slipped back to bed before she was spotted — but that, it seemed, wouldn't do. The rabbits were her job on Dr Moroni's weekly rota, which meant she had to attend to them herself in person.

Sudden anger boiled up in me as I looked at her small, tear-stained face. 'Don't worry about Dr Moroni, I'll make it right with him,' I promised. At last I managed to half-pull, half-coax her from her refuge and put my cardigan round her shoulders. 'Let's go and feed those bunnies together, how about that? Where do they live?'

Firmly and comfortingly, I held on to her. But just as we were stealing off together like conspirators down the corridor, a sound behind us made us stop — that ominous whir of electrically propelled wheels.

'What's the trouble here?'

I turned to explain what the trouble

was, in quite forceful terms. 'And I must say,' I swept on, 'some of your rules here are really quite inhuman. Poor Bridget isn't used to animals, she's new here and she's frightened — and I don't blame her at all!'

He cut me short with his exasperating 'Uh-huh. Haven't you said about enough?'

I bit my lip, still seething. Of course, I knew I shouldn't discuss patients in their presence, far less query The Haven's methods. Usually I would have been more discreet, but after the strain of this long strange day, and all the doubts nagging at me since I arrived, this final incident was just one too many.

'Here's what we'll do,' Lowell was saying briskly. 'I'll give Tubby and Cuddles their supper. You see Bridget safely back to bed. I'll speak to you both in the morning.'

'I hate him! And I want to go home,' Bridget cried, once he'd gone.

I hushed her, with a disturbing

feeling that I fully agreed. On both counts.

'Paula, don't let him get you down, my dear.' I recognised Faye Prescott's patronising but friendly voice.

'Take my advice,' she added, 'don't try stepping out of line. That's one thing Lowell won't abide.'

I was too ruffled and annoyed to find an immediate answer. She just patted my arm with condescending kindness, then hurried on to catch up with Lowell.

Suddenly, I was quite looking forward to being carpeted tomorrow for my behaviour. If Lowell Moroni smugly assumed his new assistant was too subdued, too immersed in personal problems, to become seriously involved in other battles, perhaps he was in for quite a big surprise!

3

There were strange and alien sounds in the air when I woke to my first full day at The Haven. Overnight, I had tossed and turned restlessly, my mind constantly churning. Now, broad daylight was flooding my high attic room.

The mournful cries of the seagulls were unfamiliar to me. Other cries, human and excited, sounded like children engaged in some vigorous physical activity. 'Run, Eddie, you goof, run!' someone screamed. And, 'Good old Ben, what a super hit!'

This was a respectable, small clinic for young patients too disabled and disturbed to live their lives in the normal world! On this Saturday morning at the unearthly hour of half-past seven, their lives were being lived with great enthusiasm!

I pulled aside the curtain to peer

down at the stretch of grass reserved for games. What today's game was called I couldn't be sure — it seemed like a version of rounders-cum-baseball, including Lowell in his power-driven chair with a sweat-shirt prominently lettered COACH, and Faye Prescott sporting a becoming pale-mint track-suit.

As I watched, a boy with tow-coloured, spiky hair, and a caliper on his leg — Ben, I believed — was going all-out to reach second base, his face scarlet with effort. I called quickly, 'Jeremy, hurry and put on some clothes, you're missing all the fun!'

But Jeremy, yawning dejectedly from the adjoining room, refused to move. He could run 10 times as fast as Ben without even trying, he declared, so what was the point?

'Ah, but maybe you can't hit the ball so hard,' I reasoned.

Some of Lowell's impassioned words in the briefing session last evening came back to me. 'What you can do well, do better than well — then the things you do less well can take care of themselves.'

However, this wasn't the best moment to preach a sermon to a grouchy, half-awake Jeremy still brooding about his easy-going Aunt Penny and his friend, Adam, from upstairs.

I bustled Jeremy into the bathroom — redolent of whatever French perfume Sophie, who had the neighbouring room, had applied to herself. We were both just ready for the public gaze when the breakfast bell jangled through the house.

On the way down, I was remembering what had happened last night with poor Bridget and her rabbit-feeding duties — and Lowell Moroni's arbitrary order to report to his office this morning. Well, I was ready for him! Overnight I had worked out some very plain words to express my feelings about Bridget. He wasn't going to ride rough-shod over my opinions simply because I was a newcomer!

But once seated with Jeremy at one of the red-topped tables in the dining-room in a prevailing atmosphere of scorched toast, the wind was rather drained from my sails. The ball-players were just streaming in, their complexions ruddy from the early morning air and subsequent washing of hands and faces, their voices arguing excitedly about whether Liz's fabulous hit was better than Ben's.

'Can Eddie play on our side next time, please, Dr Moroni?' someone was pleading with Lowell. A girl called Camilla with glorious ripe-corn hair and a prominent facial scar was clamouring, 'Dr Moroni, it is Lions fifteen wins and The Wolves twelve, isn't it? Ben says it's only thirteen-twelve.'

Clustering eagerly round his chair, they were quite forgetting to sheer away from my alien occupation of the corner table. I watched him laughing, sympathising, teasing and praising, in turn. Slowly there was dawning on me something I had missed in my hasty first appraisals last evening — that as well as a basis of real awe, they regarded him with something like adoration.

Even the squad who had been laying out the breakfast instead of playing weren't too upset about it, just boasting what they would do for The Lions or The Wolves when their turn came next time round.

Over the cereal bowls and scrambled eggs, someone asked whether Jeremy was to be a Lion or a Wolf. The numbers were at present uneven, so The Lions claimed him as their right.

Camilla warned him. 'And you'd better be good, 'cos we're the best!'

Jeremy stubbornly refused to show much interest, but I could see he was pleased.

After the meal, with the crockery being cleared on to trolleys under the eagle eye of Mrs Burns, I left Jeremy moodily unpacking the rest of his possessions upstairs, and kept my appointment in Dr Moroni's room.

'Come in!' His voice answered my

tap on the door.

I entered the room to find Bridget there with the doctor. The frail little girl looked no happier, and her face was blotched with tears. He was coaxing her with gentleness, 'Come on, honey, no more miseries. Can't you see the sunshine outside? How about a ride to the shops in our own little bus?'

Bridget plainly wasn't sure. But I was touched to see her brighten just a little at the sight of me.

Lowell had noticed, too, because he appealed again, 'You'll go for a nice ride, won't you — if Nurse Hastings goes along with you?'

I was doubtful about what he was letting me in for so soon. But Bridget's relieved glance really left me no choice. However, when she went off to get ready for the trip, I found the opportunity to say quite firmly what I had come to say.

'About last night — I did get a little carried away and I'm sorry about that. But I still stand by everything I said about Bridget. I do believe you can carry your strict discipline too far, especially in certain cases . . . '

He only murmured, 'Uh-huh,' while his restless hands searched the jumble of papers on his desk with impatience.

I was nettled enough to demand. 'What does 'uh-huh' mean exactly? Are you listening to me?'

Then, disconcertingly, his eyes lifted to mine. 'Sure I am. You've made a snap decision about my methods, and you don't approve.'

'I wouldn't say . . . ' I hesitated.

'Yes, you would.' Suddenly his unexpected smile flashed out. 'It's OK, Paula, I shan't hold it against you. At least you have the guts to say what you think. When you've been here longer, you'll understand better what I'm doing — and meantime, shall we let yesterday drop?

'I never make an issue out of yesterdays, it's the todays that matter. We'll put it down to over-concern on your part, and in my book that's a whole heap better than inertia. In a while you'll be a real asset to The Haven.'

I opened my mouth, then shut it again foolishly. All my pre-prepared arguments had suddenly evaporated, perhaps melted away by that disarming smile. I fumed inwardly, it was utterly unfair of this man to confuse people by being so downright obnoxious one moment and so warmly charming the next.

'The best plan for you,' he was going on, 'is to spend this week-end getting acclimatised — just look, listen, and get to know us. Next week will be time enough to start working seriously, studying my therapy sessions with the kids and so on.

'For now, just help out a little if you see someone who needs helping and, of course, you'll want to give plenty of time to Jeremy. He'll have a lot of adjusting to do, too. Maybe a new start here will help break up some of those barriers you told me about.'

I could only mumble a subdued, 'Thank you,' deeply grateful for his depth of understanding. One day, I might even get around to understanding him, too — if I remained at The Haven that long!

★ ★ ★

'All aboard! All persons for shopping on ze bus, please!' Sophie called out. She stood by the dusty yellow mini-bus, in a very tight skirt, very high heels, and a striking shade of cherry-red lipstick.

With her was a part-time assistant I hadn't met till now, a local girl whose family kept a small guest-house in St Owen, I had been told. Bright-faced and chatty, Debbie smiled at me and held out a friendly hand.

'All on ze bus,' Sophie requested again.

I bundled a sulky Jeremy and a woeful Bridget on board. I held on to her tightly, partly for comfort and partly fearing she might make a run for it. Apart from Sophie, our fellow passengers were Camilla; her friend, Angela, with a fringe of mouse-brown hair and a bad limp; and two boys, Geoff and Eddie. All were armed with business-like shopping-lists and trolleys.

'The best of the bunch,' Debbie whispered to me, 'the least troublesome individuals to unleash on the outside world.'

I took her word for it.

Our driver was an apologetic little man with sparse grey hair and a permanent expression of worry, whom the informative Debbie identified as Joe Burns.

'Not the husband of . . . ?' I whispered back, and she giggled. I wasn't surprised Mr Burns looked harassed!

Still holding Bridget's hand, I settled back to look at the passing scenery. Once away from the coast, it was a little grim and barren, I thought, unlike the smiling green Devon we had driven through yesterday. Here were granite walls and weather-beaten cottages, bracken and boulders and the far-off eerie ruin of a mine. But it had its own mysterious beauty.

'Is this what they call a town?' Jeremy was demanding in despair when a main road brought us to the outskirts of Penvor. To the London child, the Saturday bustle of the place would look vastly inadequate. Nevertheless, there was an open market and a handful of bigger stores as well as gift shops selling Cornish lucky charms and souvenirs of the nearby priory.

Mr Burns turned into the car park attached to a modest supermarket and the children began scrambling out.

'Half an hour, back here at the bus,' I agreed with Debbie and Sophie, and left them to their shopping for household supplies, while Mr Burns stayed put in his seat and lit up an evil-smelling pipe.

With Jeremy on one side and Bridget on the other, I explored all the High Street could offer in the way of postcards to send back to Penny, and Linda's family, and the Miss Coombes next door. I felt as though I were here on holiday — but I was quickly reminded that this was not so.

Bridget was soon in floods of tears at the suggestion she should buy a card to send home, wailing pitifully, 'I can't! My auntie doesn't make me go in shops! I want to go back home to my auntie!'

Bridget's troubles, of course, stemmed from the scarred, stiffened hands which were her sad legacy from the fire tragedy that had destroyed her home. She was hyper-sensitive about their blemished clumsiness. Now, unsure how to cope, I ended by just choosing a card myself and slipping it into her pocket.

Jeremy, with no such inhibitions, had picked out two comics, three tubes of sweets, and a Space-Zoomer kite. I was so wrapped up in Bridget that I paid for them all, unprotesting.

We still had some time left. The sight

of an inviting little cafe made me say with excellent intentions and precious little commonsense, 'Now this is just what we need. Ice-creams for you and a coffee for me, how about it?'

If Bridget was afraid to hand a coin over a shop counter, her fear of sitting down in public to wield a spoon was far greater. The tears started again, quite hysterically. Years ago, Nurse Hastings would doubtless have viewed this as a very minor crisis — but that was in a different world, when I was a different person . . .

'Quick, before the bus goes!' Jeremy, spurred on by the thought of losing his own treat, grabbed Bridget's arm. 'Look, someone in there is eating a super chocolate thing with pink underneath. If you can't spoon it, lick it! You have a tongue!'

It might have been Dr Moroni speaking!

Bridget was hustled into the cafe, and somehow we were sitting at a table where Jeremy ordered grandly, 'Two of them like that person's got, please.' Again, I meekly paid up. It was a small price for getting Bridget to join this impromptu party.

Jeremy was whispering to her, his temper mellowed by the Space-Zoomer and the sundae, and she actually forgot her own nightmare enough to giggle at what he was saying.

Bridget ate little, and most of that was fed to her in down-to-earth fashion by Jeremy — strictly against The Haven's principles — before he finished off the rest himself. Still, it was a victory. Far more Jeremy's than mine, but suddenly I was elated, eager to do more and pour out an account of it all to Lowell. I wanted him to approve. Despite our differences, it mattered to me what he thought of me.

'Race you to the bus! Come on, Bridget,' Jeremy was challenging her.

We found Mr Burns just loading up groceries and vegetables. Eddie and Geoff were arguing about something, and Angela had been crying. Sophie and Debbie looked harassed. Next time, I thought, I would be of more help to them.

As the bus moved off, there was suddenly a whole blossoming of new ideas I needed to discuss with Lowell Moroni.

★ ★ ★

Boiled potatoes were on the lunch menu. Likewise, cabbage. I wasn't too sure what Jeremy, whose tastes ran on chips with chips, would make of it.

'From local growers, dear, nothing to beat it,' the motherly Annie Beecher assured me, busily shepherding the diners into their places.

I mumbled, 'Yes, I'm sure.' Already I was feeling disappointed because, on my return from Penvor, I'd found Lowell tied up with a new patient. After lunch, I hoped, he might have time for me.

Meanwhile, the meal was proving a bit of a disaster. Several children

— egged on by the deceptively cherub-faced Tony — began squabbling over something and Sophie's excited efforts to separate them only made matters worse.

There was much pushing and shoving, and in the end someone was barged forcibly against one of the tables just as Mrs Burns, in the inevitable navy overall and cast-iron coiffeur, was handing out steaming platefuls from her trolley. Lunches and crockery were strewn around the floor. There were dismayed words from Mrs Beecher and much Gallic hand-waving from Sophie.

Finally, Mrs Burns herself ended the brief lapse into anarchy, by standing over the culprits with a soup-ladle while they cleared up the mess.

'I shall be telling Dr Moroni about this,' she warned all of us dourly. 'And I shall be giving him in my notice. There's a limit to what human flesh and blood can stand, that's what I say!'

My attention was diverted then to Jeremy, as I realised he hadn't touched a mouthful. He announced that the meal was 'Foul and yukky!'

I shushed him hastily before Mrs Burns turned her gaze our way.

'Aunt Penny and me always went to Bert's Chip Bar on Saturdays,' Jeremy grumbled on. 'Then I rode my bike with Adam in the park — '

'We'll go out later,' I tried to tempt him. 'I'm sure Bridget will come, too.'

But he only went on mourning his absent friend and left-alone-bike. In fact, I had left it behind deliberately feeling that the sight of him racing about on it might be unkind to disabled patients unable to ride themselves.

It proved the final straw for him when rice pudding arrived for dessert. He jumped up and marched out of the room, clumping off upstairs to sulk. The hopeful signs of this morning's shopping trip weren't lasting long.

'Sorry, domestic problems,' I told Annie, and followed in his wake. On the way, I passed Faye Prescott coming out of Lowell's office, cool and elegant as ever, and she asked pleasantly, 'How's it going, Paula?'

'Everything's fine, thanks,' I told her stiffly. Somehow I couldn't bring myself to ask her if Lowell was free yet.

Upstairs, Jeremy was sprawled on his bed, determined to be miserable. It didn't help to explain patiently again why his bike was back in London. Nor to point out that The Haven provided other amusements and many new friends.

'It's just not fair,' he complained bitterly. 'Why do I have to live in a hospital when there's nothing wrong with me? If you want to work here it's all right for you, but why did you make me come with you? You don't really want me, so you could have left me back at home.'

He didn't know how hurtful these words were. Of course, he was only a child, and had no way of understanding what had happened to the two of us. Although we played a polite game of pretence that we were a family, to him I was a hollow image of the mother he used to know. To me he was a stranger I could never quite reach — and a constant reminder of the frightening blank in my life.

'Jeremy, listen to me.' Shakily, I sat down on the bed beside him. 'You mustn't say things like that! Of course I want you. I wouldn't dream of coming all this way and leaving you behind.'

He paid little heed, as he delivered the ultimate blow. 'Well, I bet my dad wouldn't ever have made me come here.'

For a moment then I sat quite still and silent, just staring at him, at his grey accusing eyes.

For a brief while all the new impressions of The Haven had been enough to fill my mind, but now my own familiar nightmare of loss and confusion was flooding back. Perhaps, indeed, Jeremy was right. Was it really unkind and unfair to go on trying to tie his life to mine?

He was at the window now, gazing

out into the pleasant afternoon sunshine. I made a sudden effort and joined him there.

'Well, we won't mope in here all day. We haven't explored yet, let's go for a walk and take that Space-Hopper kite you bought this morning. It'll be windy by the sea.'

'It's a Zoomer, not a Hopper,' he corrected me pityingly. But he did at least look brighter at the mention of an outing.

I hustled him downstairs before he could change his mind.

In the lobby I told a passing Annie Beecher, 'We're just off to explore.'

She looked at me with a little concern and asked, 'Sure you're all right, dear? If I was you, I'd just stroll down to the nearest beach. Keep left and it's not far — nice and quiet, too. The other way there's gorgeous scenery, but it's quite a tramp.'

I thanked her and went on hurrying Jeremy outside while the going was good.

The lane to the left, with sun on our faces and a stiff breeze lifting the vividly red-gold hair we shared, led us indeed quite easily through a cleft in the cliffs to a tiny, unspoiled beach. It was deserted save for gulls soaring and swooping over the blue-green water that broke into white spray against half-submerged rocks. A fringe of sand was scattered with boulders, rock-pools, shells, and fronds of stranded seaweed.

'Oh, yes, this is great. I bet my Zoomer will go into orbit along here!' Jeremy exclaimed.

For me, this sudden confrontation with the seashore was shattering. Until now I really had just hoped the fresh air might blow away some of our troubles, not really thinking where we were walking to. But now, all at once, the near sight and sound and smell of the sea filled my senses.

Scarcely aware of forming my horror into words, I heard myself shout, 'Jeremy, let's go back! I don't like it here!'

I heard the child answer in annoyed protest, 'But we've only just this minute got here.'

'It's all right, Paula,' another voice said. 'Just hang on. I'll be with you in a moment.'

I looked round at Lowell, somehow managing the rough, steep path in his power-driven chair. His presence seemed like the answer to a prayer.

★ ★ ★

He wasn't alone, but had in tow a boy I hadn't seen before, an overweight roly-poly child peering through glasses and huddled in a hooded anorak. With a brisk normality that brought my wandering senses straight back to the present, he introduced me.

'Nurse Hastings, I'd like you to meet Morgan. Morgan is staying with us a while. He's just arrived, and I'm showing him the sights.'

From pure instinct, I held out a hand and muttered, 'Hello, Morgan, it's going to be nice having you with us.'

'Sure it is.' Lowell smiled approvingly, ignoring the boy's shrinking silence. He looked round at Jeremy, who had drifted nearer curiously, struggling with some tangle-up on his kite. 'Hi, Jeremy! Do we have a hitch on the launch-pad?'

'It won't fly right,' Jeremy agreed grudgingly. He hesitated, then surrendered his treasure into the strong, inviting hand.

'Uh-huh. Looks like we'll have to hold the count-down. So right now, why don't you look along the beach with Morgan and see what you can both find for our competition next week? The prettiest shell, or pebble. Super prizes!'

Jeremy had already opened his mouth to protest, no doubt, that it wasn't his job to look after new patients. However, meeting Lowell's dark, compelling gaze, he asked lamely instead, 'What sort of prizes?'

'Win one, and you'll find out!'

With a resigned sigh, Jeremy turned to say to the newcomer, 'Sounds a bit stupid, but shall we have a go?' Morgan seemed only to disappear farther into his coat.

In the end, Jeremy grabbed his arm and, without ceremony, marched him off. 'I bet the prizes are no good, anyway,' he was saying gruffly, as he dragged the silent Morgan — probably two years older and at least three times his size — towards a promising rock pool.

'A sad case. You want to hear about it?' Lowell came closer to me, lowering his voice. 'A few years back the kid had a bad fall from a step-ladder, while his mother was hanging curtains. She blamed herself completely — even after the broken bones healed she kept on treating him as a helpless baby, never letting him lift a finger, filling him up with candies.

'So now he's petrified about going to school and getting laughed at, hyper-sensitive about his size — he scarcely says a word, just tries to hide behind layers of clothing as some sort of screen. I think we can help Morgan, but it won't be easy.'

At another moment that absorbing history would have held all my attention. But now, the woes of this quaint-looking boy took second place to the accusations of my own son still aching in my heart. Though I had turned my back on that frightening sea, its nearness still possessed me with a terror I couldn't control.

'Come on, then. Tell me,' the voice beside me invited, suddenly warm and gentle.

I didn't question how Lowell knew the agony behind my silence, nor how that invitation could suddenly bring words pouring out in a relieving flood, just as they did at our first meeting. I half-sobbed, 'Oh, I — I've had such an awful time!'

'I know. I can see. Tell me.'

'I think Jeremy hates me for bringing him here.'

'I see. When Annie told me where you were headed, I followed on. OK. don't be frightened any more, just tell me about it.'

I told him all there was to tell, how my fear couldn't be controlled when I was near the sea. It was as though a great pent-up burden of pain and fear found relief in the telling.

He said at last, 'We'll find the answers for you, Paula. I promise you. It may take a while, but we'll work it out.'

I looked into the square, dark face, with its own strange mingling of strength and weakness.

'Feeling better?' he asked. 'Then hadn't you better get along the beach there and keep an eye on the boys?'

Glancing round at the two figures, now quite far off at the water's edge, I was amazed at the distance they had covered. But though my sheer panic had been soothed, enough still remained to anchor my feet in the sand and make my heart race. I couldn't bring myself to approach closer to the sea.

'Please,' I said shakily, 'I — I don't want to go near the water, let's just call them back.'

As loudly as I could, I shouted to them. The breeze and the tide carried the sound away. Jeremy didn't lift his head.

Lowell said, 'It's OK, I'll go after them.'

To my shame, I didn't protest. I just stood there watching him.

Whoever had designed that long-suffering chair of his hadn't expected an occupant to give it such a very testing work-out as this. Yet Lowell whirred along, without tipping himself out, or any major disaster, until he was quite near the boys. Then, right at the water's edge, the incvitable happened. His wheels stuck fast in the wet sand. An oncoming wave showered him with spray as the wheels settled deeper.

The physical helplessness of this so-dynamic man came painfully home to me as he shouted to the boys, 'Rescue! Heave ho, my hearties! First man aboard gets the salvage rights!'

Still I just stood there and watched as they hurried to help him. Jeremy was actually laughing, and even Morgan's unnatural gravity gave way just a little. He even pushed his trouser legs a few inches up very white, podgy legs to join the gleeful Jeremy in splashing barefoot to the rescue.

By the time their combined heaving and tugging and the chair's over-worked mechanism had shifted a half-drenched Lowell a little way up the beach, I had forced my paralysed legs into movement. By now the boys had run off to retrieve their shells and pebbles. Lowell was mopping himself up with an inadequate handkerchief.

'Are — are you all right? I'm so sorry, it was my fault for being so stupid. And I didn't even come to help you.'

'Don't worry about it.' He cut short my apologies.

But I did worry. I was colder than he

was, standing there on the sun-warmed sand and shivering uncontrollably — until suddenly a hand found mine and held it fast, and, by some strange magic, gave me warmth and courage.

'Don't worry,' he repeated. 'Give it time. Just give it time.'

That handclasp gave me something more than courage; it made my pulses race. Now it wasn't only the recurring nightmare of the water that held me dazed and speechless. I clawed strands of bright hair from my face, and all at once felt suddenly shy in his presence.

We must have looked a strange procession on our way back. Morgan had shrunk back into his muffled-up, silent self, and I was equally quiet.

Jeremy, prancing along, gleefully assured Lowell he deserved a medal for the gallant rescue because it was just in the nick of time. 'There was a huge great shark just swimming ashore to get you, all grey and horrible, with simply hundreds of teeth!'

'I know,' Lowell said gravely. 'But it

wasn't really a shark. Just Mrs Burns out for a paddle.'

When Jeremy laughed, the sun on my face at last grew warm.

★   ★   ★

Our evening meal was less eventful than lunch. With Lowell present this time, even though he chatted and joked, no one misbehaved under his quick and watchful eyes.

There were no longer two spare seats at the table where I sat with Jeremy. Bridget had been moved to one and Morgan occupied the other, his glasses glimmering mutely across at me. So I was already beginning to fill some sort of role in the life of The Haven. Despite all today's trials, that delighted me.

The meal wasn't easy, with Bridget needing encouragement for each mouthful and Morgan silent as a zombie. I tried praising him for rescuing Dr Moroni, and was amazed when he mumbled, 'King Canute.'

I agreed readily. 'He did look like King Canute! I hadn't thought of that, I'm not too good on history.'

He supplied, with monosyllabic attention to detail, other facts about Canute.

Still more surprised, I made a mental note to tell Lowell. However, there was no chance straight away, even when the dining-room began emptying. Faye Prescott had switched from her table to his and was in the midst of some lengthy anecdote.

Nor could I tell him later, because a slide show was being held in the big hall. Not really so big, it still boasted rows of chairs facing a small stage. Tonight a screen and projector were in readiness. There was a hum of chatter as the chairs filled up.

'Right folks, settle down,' Lowell ordered. 'We'll start with a selection of work by the camera club. Lights off, Annie. Right, Faye, roll 'em.'

His chair, still a trifle sandy, was beside Faye, who was acting as projectionist. From there he gave us a commentary on the colourful local views: lanes and villages, Penvor Priory and, of course, the sea — rocks and breakers, and a sombre beauty spot called The Maiden's Pool, whose waters were replenished every high tide via subterranean tunnels in the cliffs.

'Supposed to be bottomless,' he informed us dramatically. 'The legends say a girl drowned there one night while waiting for her faithless sweetheart.'

Ben and Geoff clamoured to know if the luckless maiden still haunted the spot, hoping for tales of a corpse-like face afloat amid trails of weed-entangled hair.

Lowell moved on hastily to safer themes. First, a library of natural history subjects. Then, various New York scenes, many taken by himself. They included a surprising shot of a modest 'Diner,' where a coloured sign advised passers-by to 'Try Ma Moroni's Jumbo Burgers' while Lowell was posed on a chair in the doorway in a chef's hat. The audience reacted to that with delighted giggles.

'No,' Faye told a hopeful Tony, 'Dr Moroni's mother doesn't fry up real elephants!' She, at least, seemed unsurprised by this glimpse into Lowell's background. 'You know,' she observed to him, 'when I had my American holiday I may have passed right by your mother's place.'

In the big, dimmed room, I saw her smiling at him, her head bent near his as she added even more confidentially, 'We really should invite her over very soon for a holiday.'

By now I was frowning quite darkly at the screen. I wasn't happy that Miss Prescott so obviously had other interests at The Haven beyond the children's welfare. Also, there had flashed into my mind all Hugh Egerton's vague accusations about Lowell, as a man and as a doctor — which at the time I had dismissed out of hand. Now, I could no longer deny that Lowell Moroni had indeed a rather incredible background for a medical man, what with his opera-singing and his burgers.

The next slide really served to emphasise that, and his grunt of annoyance indicated it had arrived on the screen by accident. In fact, it was an attractive picture: a small group sitting outside a sunny Mediterranean villa with, in the forefront, an older, whiter-haired version of the distinguished tenor Guilio Moroni, Lowell's grandfather, whose portrait hung in his room here. Beside the old man was a slim, raven-haired boy gazing up into his face. His grandfather had a rather sad face, I thought. The passage of years, of fame and acclaim, didn't seem to have brought him much happiness.

'So the great man isn't above making a hit with the local children,' Faye said.

'That's right!' Lowell cut her short. 'OK, this is the end of the show. Lights, Annie. You all have jobs to do before bedtime, so just see they're done.'

I doubted if the entertainment was meant to finish quite so abruptly. But for me, the end hadn't come too soon. After this long, long day I was exhausted.

Luckily, Jeremy was tired enough, too, to fall asleep as soon as he was in bed. I tried to complete an unfinished letter to Penny, but soon found it was hopeless. It would have to be done tomorrow. There was a guilty thought in my mind as I fell into bed. I had promised to ring Hugh today!

Well, I certainly couldn't do it now. The delayed phone call, like the tardy letter, would have to be tomorrow.

The next day began with the sound of early Sunday hymn singing. As Jeremy had declined joining in the game, I could hardly expect any enthusiasm about the choir.

Doggedly homesick as ever, apparently he intended moping in bed all day. It seemed like a case for firmness.

'We'll explore the village, we haven't seen it yet,' I told him. 'Yes, I know Aunt Penny always bought you an ice-lolly on Sunday mornings. Hurry and get ready, maybe we'll find some shops open.'

Due to all this, I arrived for breakfast just as the room was emptying. 'Sorry,' I apologised to Lowell, whose glance at his watch was a silent lecture on punctuality. 'I had trouble with Jeremy. I thought I'd take him to explore St Owen this morning, if I'm not needed here?'

'Sure.' He nodded. 'I told you to devote yourself to him first. Tell him his Space-Skimmer is nearly OK now.'

'Zoomer,' I corrected absently. Those black searching eyes seemed as usual to see right through me, and I wondered how much they really saw. The touch of his hand on mine yesterday was like a dream now.

'Oh, yes, and I wanted to tell you about Morgan,' I said, remembering. 'He said down on the beach yesterday you were like King Canute sitting on his throne at the water's edge and ordering the waves to recede!'

'You got him talking? That's fine! King Who?'

'Canute. Ten hundred and something. Morgan even knew the date, so . . .'

'So he was interested enough to remember it. That's just the sort of lead we need. I'll arrange a general knowledge quiz one evening with plenty of history questions specially for him. That should give his self-confidence a boost. Good work, Paula.'

Lowell's approval glowed in me. On the strength of it I found myself asking, 'Shall I take Morgan along to the village with us? And Bridget, too?'

After yesterday, I doubted if he would trust me. But he nodded quite casually. 'You do that. Just don't go too far with them.' On his way across to the door, he glanced round just once. 'This screwball Canute. What happened to him?'

'He got wet feet,' I said.

Half an hour ago, I had felt I would never laugh again.

When I gathered the children together and found their coats, Lowell was at the door to wave us off with a cheery, 'Have a good time, guys.'

However, it wasn't a particularly successful outing. St Owen, straggling its houses and two or three inns and modest hotels around a small harbour and a handful of boats, was picturesque, of course, but on this greyish morning there was little to see or do. A few shops were open to sell sweets and Cornish souvenirs.

Jeremy, who liked his seasides bright, brash, and busy, summed up. 'I've been to some boring dumps, but this is about the worst of the lot!' He was just about as disgusted with St Owen as with the company he was once again keeping — Bridget snivelling into her sleeve in habitual misery, and Morgan puffing along in the rear like a bespectacled barrel in mummy-like swathings of scarves.

I ended up parking the ill-assorted trio on a seat outside the little Post

Office with a picnic of crisps and chocolate, while I went into an adjoining phone-box. From there, I dialled Penny's flat three times without result.

I tried Hugh's London number as well. There the answering-machine was switched on, and I said a few stilted words to await his return. He could be away somewhere, of course. Penny would be out with Kevin. I couldn't expect them to sit over their telephones for me.

Meantime, I had a good view of the children and it struck me that for the first time, Jeremy seemed interested in something, talking and pointing an animated finger. The object of his attention was the local bus pulling in nearby.

As I left the phone booth, I caught just a few words of what he was holding forth about in superior fashion to his companions. He was saying that the bus would probably link up with the railway. It would be easy to find out about main line trains through to London — which was where his Aunt Penny and all his friends lived, and where he should still be living, too.

A completely new dread shuddered through me. He surely wouldn't try running away back home!

Aware now of my presence, he was asking very innocently for more crisps. I dared not mention what I had heard, or half-heard. If I had misunderstood, it would only put the idea into his receptive mind.

Wishing now I hadn't come out at all, I bustled them back towards The Haven. My head was throbbing with anxiety and weariness. When we arrived back, the atmosphere of Sunday lunch made me realise I couldn't eat, nor cope with Jeremy not eating.

'Oh, Paula, there you are, dear!' Mrs Beecher pounced on me almost before I was inside, clearly agog with excitement. 'You don't know what you missed while you were out. I took a phone call for you — and do you know, it was Hugh Egerton.'

'Oh. Yes. What did Hugh want?' I asked.

'You call him Hugh?' Debbie said in amazement. 'Do you really know him well?'

'Paula, could you get us a signed photo?'

It seemed as though the whole staff of The Haven were demanding how, where, and when I came to know Hugh, and whether he looked as fabulous off the screen as on it. I had to get away by myself to rest. It was the lunch bell that saved me.

'I'm rather tired. If I lie down for a little while, could you see Jeremy has his lunch, please?' I appealed to the kindly Annie, who knew that I had been seriously ill for a long time.

She assured me she would, and he could watch TV afterwards with the others. In her concern, she wanted to ply me with aspirins, tea, and hot-water bottles. Just as I escaped, I managed to ask, 'Did Hugh leave a message?'

'I'm ever so sorry, dear, yes, he did,' she confessed. 'But I was so bowled over, I just couldn't take it in!'

I said it didn't matter. Upstairs, mercifully, all was very quiet.

* * *

Never expecting to sleep, I must have dozed through sheer fatigue. When I opened my eyes, I was aware that the draught from the window had thoroughly chilled me.

I slid stiffly off the bed to shut it. It was then, looking down from this high vantage point, that I saw a large black car just pulling up in the drive. Perhaps the sound of it had roused me, or some sixth sense given me warning. I knew this car. I knew the driver just emerging, the tall, fair-haired man quietly taking stock of all around him. Annie and Debbie must be busy or by now they would have rushed outside hysterical with delight.

Yet my own reaction, as I scrubbed

the heaviness of sleep from my eyes, wasn't of undiluted joy. This visit was far too soon! I hadn't yet had time, in my short stay at The Haven, to solve the problem of Hugh's marriage proposal. And it was unfair to expect me to have found my feet so soon in this new environment.

Hurrying downstairs, I realised what a bad moment he had picked for first impressions of the place. Outside, a wellington-booted 'garden-tidying detail' were drearily busy in a drizzle of rain, doing their best to look like orphans in a storm.

Bridget was crying in the porch. Indoors, Tony had started some noisy rumpus, while the grim tones of Mrs Burns drifted equally loudly from the kitchen regions, demanding which of her helpers had left the refrigerator awash with fruit juice. Last but not least, Delilah the cat and one of her kittens were hopefully angling in the fish tank, poised between a goldfish banquet and a watery grave.

'Hugh, what a lovely surprise!' I ran out to greet him, hoping to divert his attention. A little late for that. The sternness of his face relaxed only a little as he looked at me.

'Hello, Paula. Sorry I'm later than I promised. You did get my message?'

'Er — sort of.'

'I have to see someone in Exeter tomorrow, so the chance of seeing you was too good to miss. I've been very anxious about you.' The growing depth of his concern was changing his usual quiet courtesy into bluntness. 'Do you know you look like a ghost?'

I had thought the sea air had, in fact, given me a little colour. 'I — I'm just a little tired,' I stammered. 'Will you come inside?'

'I can see you're tired. Have they been overworking you?'

'I'm not working at all yet,' I admitted foolishly.

'You're not? Then how will you feel when you do begin? What's wrong with the little girl in the doorway?'

'Oh, that's Bridget. She just cries all the time.'

'I see. And how is Jeremy? Where is he?'

I had to admit that I wasn't sure where he was at the moment.

'I see,' he said again, then came to a sudden halt on the path, from where the children's shouts indoors were audible.

'Let's not pretend, Paula. You had good intentions, but you made a mistake coming here.' The velvet voice had just a hint in it of the steel I'd heard so alarmingly once before. 'So will you come back to London with me tomorrow, before you get embroiled any more in this shambles? The sooner you're away from here, the better!'

Miserably, I shook my head. 'I can't do that. I still don't believe it was a mistake. And — I'm committed here, I can't let Dr Moroni down.'

'We'll see about that.' His voice hardened still more. 'I've already warned you that your loyalty to him could be another mistake. Will you take me in now to see him? I'm not leaving here till I've talked to him.'

My head was beginning to whirl, as it did at any crisis. But at this point, the situation was snatched out of my hands. There was an approaching click of high heels, a waft of perfume, and a new presence took charge.

'Mr Egerton, we're very honoured to have you here. I heard you rang Paula, but I couldn't quite believe it. I'm Faye Prescott, I look after the children's education,' she introduced herself as she came swanning out from the house looking, I thought quite viciously, as though she'd stepped out of a glossy magazine. 'Lowell will be back any minute. Do come inside and let me show you round while we're waiting.'

I trailed along behind them. Bridget was still crying, Tony still shouting, the cats were probably still fishing — unless they had fallen in. I felt shaky with anger and humiliation.

'Are you here to give us lots of

publicity in your Good Causes and Bad Causes TV programme?' Faye asked. 'Only good publicity, I hope.'

The words gripped me. If Hugh really chose to end my rebellious presence here, he had the means to do both Lowell and Lowell's beloved Haven a ruinous amount of damage.

4

'Well, you certainly do have very good facilities here for the children,' Hugh had to agree, just a shade grudgingly.

Faye gave him her bright smile. 'You're not actually seeing us at our best, is he, Paula? Not on this horrid rainy day — and the kids seem to have horrid rainy tempers to match.'

I mumbled agreement, as she was deigning to notice my existence. Until now I had trailed along behind while she gave him a tour of all there was to see. But I had to grant Faye had style, she was never lost for an answer — and she certainly had presented the place in its best possible light at a rather bad moment.

'You haven't seen the tower wing, but there's not much in it yet, except paint pots and step-ladders,' she was telling the visitor now. 'Normally it's kept locked up. Originally it was built as an observatory — but Lowell intends turning it into an arts centre this summer. And he'll do it. He gets things done.'

Hugh didn't dispute that. All along he had accepted quietly whatever he was told, though I suspected he was saving his questions for Dr Moroni in due time. Meanwhile, of course, his presence hadn't gone unnoticed. Mrs Beecher, Debbie, and the others had been made happy with autographs and a few words to each in Hugh's quietly charming way. That always happened wherever he went. I should be used to it by now.

We had just sat down in Lowell's office to wait for him — after Faye had braved a visit to the kitchen to request tea — when The Haven's chief at last made an appearance. He had been out with a few members of the camera club making the best of the dreary afternoon.

As they came up the drive laden with

their equipment, I saw Hugh peering through the window, looking a little startled. I remembered my own first glimpse of Lowell, the contrast of the erect dark head and the power-driven wheelchair.

'It'll be a lovely surprise for him to find you here, Mr Egerton,' Faye said with a smile.

'I hope so,' Hugh remarked drily.

I dared not look at him, nor even around this room that so reflected its owner, with its heaped-up desk and the open piano, and that striking family portrait of his grandfather on the wall. I was beginning to shake in rising apprehension.

Yet perhaps it was foolish to fear some sort of earth-stopping scene. I should have trusted Hugh more and realised he had his own way of doing things. In a moment, he was rising to offer a hand with quiet, impeccable courtesy as Faye performed the introductions.

'Lowell, we've been waiting for you.

Here's a most distinguished caller, do I really need to name names?'

'Sure you don't. Hi!' Lowell greeted the visitor, inevitably. 'Excuse me not getting up, it can be done, but it takes a while. You came down to see Paula?'

'I'm very glad to make your acquaintance, Dr Moroni. Yes, I was in the vicinity — and I'd heard so much about The Haven, I wanted to see it all for myself.'

I witnessed their civil but guarded handshake. At present they were chatting pleasantly enough. The location was beautiful, they agreed. The weather was disappointing for the time of year. Then Lowell said less impersonally he was sure I would be a helpful asset to The Haven. 'And I hope I can help her, too — health-wise and memory-wise — once she settles down with us.'

'Paula has already had advice about her loss of memory. Specialised advice.'

'Uh-huh. It hasn't done much for her yet, has it? I can only do better.'

'Possibly, but it could also be very

unwise to meddle. Extremely unwise.'

A respite came then as Mrs Burns brought in refreshments, her grim face wearing a smile. She even asked the visitor sweetly if she could bring him anything else. The age of miracles wasn't past — when Hugh was around to work them.

While Faye gracefully dealt with the tea-cups, Lowell commented, 'A heart of gold, our Mrs B! Not always a barrel of laughs, and her menu is sometimes a hammer and chisel job — but if ever she acts on the notice she hands me in every week, The Haven will probably fold up around her.'

'Ah. Interesting you should say that,' Hugh remarked. 'I've just looked round your set-up here and it's most impressive — but I believe your previous Haven actually did fold up?'

'It did. Staff problems chiefly. All sorts of stupid hiccups.'

'Financial hiccups for instance?'

'Those, too.' Lowell grimaced expressively. 'But whatever rumours you may have heard, that was yesterday — and yesterdays aren't important, it's today that's important. OK? What else would you like to know?'

His usual adage, of course, which had always sounded so fiercely and irresistibly positive. I couldn't explain why it failed to sound that way now instead of just vague and evasive.

An unruffled Hugh had plenty more to say about things that interested him, particularly how successful the treatment programmes for the children were proving. Lowell admitted brusquely that if Liz returned home now she would still have her tantrums, and Ben would become immobile again, and Sarah would revert to her fixed despair — because more time was needed, much more patience and study and unstinted determination.

Again, that pet theme of his on which he could hold forth so volubly and earnestly. Only today Hugh's shrewd, searching questions seemed to inhibit his flow of words. Nothing came over the way I wanted it to come over, the way I wanted Hugh to hear it.

But there was worse to follow. After Faye had reluctantly departed to supervise her Sunday 'letters home' session, Hugh turned his attention to the portrait over the piano. Obviously, he had been doing his homework quite thoroughly. He asked about Grandfather Moroni, the former star of La Scala and other great opera houses around the world. Where was he living now? When had Lowell last seen him?

'I haven't seen him in months. We write sometimes,' he replied briefly.

'I heard him sing once. Oh, after his retirement, of course — but I happened to be in Rome when he gave a charity concert. The reception they gave him was quite incredibly moving . . . Is he interested at all in your Haven project?'

'He's interested,' Lowell said carefully. 'From a distance.'

'Perhaps that's wise. Wasn't there once a colourful newspaper account of a public argument between the two of you — when he had you ejected from the theatre? Oh, forgive me for mentioning that, I suppose it counts as just another yesterday?'

Lowell's black eyes glowered at him. 'All right, we fight like starved alley-cats, apart from a good pair of lungs and some explosive Italian blood, we don't have much in common!'

'Ah,' Hugh murmured. He was so well used to asking the right questions, dropping the right hints. I just wondered, miserably and angrily, exactly what he was trying to prove.

Whatever it was, he had Lowell on edge and unhappy. When a moment later poor Sophie peeped in to request help saying, 'Please, Eddie feels very bad after all ze wet garden work in all ze wet rain!' — she received short shrift.

'Nonsense,' Lowell snapped at her, 'haven't you learned yet that's Eddie's way of gaining attention and we just ignore him?'

Sophie flushed with humiliation in front of the visitor. But as she retreated,

Lowell changed his mind. He probably realised this was a perfect cue for escape.

'Well, Eddie did have a cough last week — so maybe I'd better take a look at him. Sorry about this!' He held out a farewell hand to Hugh. 'You'll be gone by the time I'm through. I daresay your time is as precious as mine.'

The second handshake was briefer and distinctly chillier than the first.

* * *

'The nearest he could manage to throwing me out,' Hugh commented.

We were alone now in the big room. I was still shaken by these last moments — and indeed by Hugh's presence here out of the blue, by our argument about my returning to London as he wished — and most of all the appalling thought that if he chose to harm Lowell and The Haven it was well within his power.

'Hugh, did you have to go on and on asking all those questions? It was so embarrassing,' I muttered.

'The questions weren't embarrassing. The lack of straightforward answers was.'

'He answered you. Every single thing you asked.'

'Certainly. He has a quick mind — and quite a lot of personal charisma, as I imagined he would. Paula, we've talked enough about Dr. Moroni, let's talk about you,' he said quietly. 'Have you thought better of staying on here?'

I shook my head. 'Please understand, I have to try to finish what I've started.'

'Very well. Stay a few more days, get it out of your system.' He looked at me, his face stern. 'But I'm not satisfied with this place — and you know when I'm not satisfied I don't just let things lie, don't you?'

Indeed I knew. That, and his integrity, had got him where he was today. The winning charm and manner were superficial assets along the way. He was a man to revere — or to dread.

And at this moment his warning

about The Haven seemed to me like a huge and darkly-looming threat. I could find no more words. I was utterly weary.

'Paula, darling.' The warmth of his gentle protecting arms was around me. I heard his voice again, very close to me. 'Don't look so worried. The very last thing I want is to make you unhappy. But your happiness and your health mean so much to me — and can't you see that's why I want you away from this place, because they're both at risk here?'

I couldn't answer that, either, with his warm lips silencing mine. I held on to him. The long, clinging kiss clouded and soothed my struggling mind.

'I have to go now,' he said softly. 'But I hate leaving you. Why not just get in the car — and leave all the rest to me?'

I had only to say one word and he would take me away from all the troubles and joys of The Haven — from the work I was trying to do, the new start I was trying to make. Away from my brief, bewildering relationship with Lowell Moroni . . .

I struggled to concentrate on something else Hugh was telling me. Maybe I didn't feel like returning to London just yet. I really did need fresh horizons — but there were other alternatives to The Haven. He had mentioned to me before an elderly aunt of his who lived in a sleepy village in the Kent countryside. Miss Grace Egerton had for many years devoted her life to caring for Hugh and his father, the Rev John Egerton, following the early death of Hugh's mother.

Through Hugh's boyhood she had been a second mother to him. When the Rev Egerton eventually retired from his parish, his sister nursed him during years of declining health until a final and fatal stroke. After that, she moved to her present home. I knew Hugh had a deep regard for her.

Now the old lady's own health was frail. Despite a fiercely independent nature, she would welcome some companionship and help — and obviously the company of an ex-nurse would be best of all. Especially if that person soon would belong to the family, anyway . . .

I couldn't pretend to misunderstand. Of course, I hadn't yet agreed to Hugh's proposal of marriage — but I hadn't refused, either.

'Will you promise to think about staying a while with Aunt Grace?' he was asking.

I promised. I felt the last pressure of his hand on mine before the car moved off.

★ ★ ★

When giving Hugh my promise to think about his proposition, I had meant to keep it. But over the days following his visit, I did little productive thinking. I was just too tired, mentally and physically. My first spells of duty at The Haven proved engrossing, exhausting, utterly draining my emotions and my strength.

All my spare hours were spent simply resting, or trying — mostly in vain — to keep track of Jeremy. There were times when I felt Hugh was right, that I shouldn't be here pretending I was a whole person who could live a whole life. I came very near to admitting it to him during one of his daily phone calls asking me how I was.

As yet, I was merely a very minor cog in The Haven machine, doing simple basic things like helping the most disabled children at bedtime or bathtime, or supervising their leisure activities. Years ago, it would have been child's play to the competent Nurse Hastings people said I used to be. Now, as though these demanding days weren't enough, I was also wrestling with atrocious nights: spells of aching wakefulness, fleeting sleep that brought horrific dreams — always my old nightmare of storm-racked seas and a man's choked voice calling my name.

The sound was with me still now in

broad daylight, because last night's dreams had been the worst yet. This morning my blood still ran cold at the thought of them. Despite all the activity of The Haven around me, I felt so much alone. I had been here just a week, and I doubted if I could face another week. I was very, very near to giving up. Perhaps even for Jeremy's sake I should give up — because he was getting more restless and resentful every day, with most of the resentment aimed at me.

The breakfast routine was over, and the children were in class with Faye Prescott — Jeremy with them under strong and sulky protest, even though I kept repeating it was a temporary measure until I'd chosen a school in Penvor. Apart from being on hand for the mid-morning break, my time was my own until lunch.

I wandered out into the fresh air. After a grey start, the sky was fast clearing. From an old stone seat against an ivy-clad wall, there was a panoramic view of The Haven's grounds and gardens.

But I couldn't look at it for long. The call of a wheeling gull plunged me back yet again into last night's dream — and I hid my face in my hands.

'Hi!' a voice said.

I raised my head. I was aware now of the whir of an electric wheelchair.

Lowell parked neatly beside me.

'This is my free time, I'm not on duty till later,' I told him hastily.

I hadn't really seen him alone since Hugh's traumatic visit. But from afar, I had watched him at work, so firmly in command of the establishment. I thought that in the main, he was wonderful with the children, though on occasions I still felt he was too harsh; while with the staff he was mostly exacting and impersonal. He even kept Faye at arm's length.

Already this morning we had argued, again concerning little Bridget Poole — who'd arrived late for breakfast so miserable and red-eyed that I'd tried to smuggle her in unnoticed. It hadn't worked.

'All right, you're off duty,' he was saying now. 'But do you mind not looking so dismal? It's against the rules here — especially in full view of the gates and the road. You'll give the place a bad name!'

All at once my blood was starting to boil, a reaction he not infrequently aroused.

'Dr Moroni, I'm not one of your unfortunate patients, and I'm not going to be bullied! And — and,' I finished hotly, 'if you'd ever been married then left alone — and had a son who hates the sight of you — perhaps you might be more understanding!'

'What makes you so sure the same sort of thing hasn't ever happened to me? I was married, too, Mrs Hastings, only I prefer to forget it. I also have a son. My Luke is way ahead of your Jeremy when it comes to good, honest loathing.'

'I'm very sorry, I — I had no idea,' I

150

could only apologise weakly.

'Of course you didn't. I don't spread the story around. But as we have something in common, I'll tell it to you — if you're interested?'

I wasn't just interested, I was utterly amazed. He had always seemed to me to be a person wholly self-sufficient, far apart from the domestic entanglements besetting other people.

He was, as I had guessed, of Italian/American parentage. He had little memory of his father, who had died when he was small. From the first discovery that the Moroni voice was emerging in another generation, his famous grandfather had plunged him into musical training so he could follow in the great man's operatic footsteps. Yet, despite his obvious gifts, Lowell's heart was never wholly in it. He yearned to study medicine, something Guilio Moroni couldn't or wouldn't understand. So relations between the ageing, deeply-disappointed singer and the wilful boy were stormy all along.

The result was that Lowell for some years was torn between two goals, getting nowhere with either. During this time, while staying with his mother's family in New York and resignedly studying music at his grandfather's command and expense, he met and married a young girl from California. As he described her, I knew that he had once loved her very much.

But Rita definitely saw herself as the wife of a rising star of the New York Metropolitan Opera, not just a run-of-the-mill physician; however, this conflict was temporarily put aside while she bore Lowell's child.

Bianca Maria, with her mother's beauty and her father's dark eyes, had been born terribly handicapped. This, somehow, became a turning point for Lowell, deciding him to abandon music and plunge into medical studies. Inevitably, this caused a deep family rift, not only with Rita, but with his grandfather.

The sad, early death of little Bianca

only partly united the bereaved parents in their sorrow. Rita was soon berating Lowell, in one of their many flaming quarrels, that he could by now have been famous and wealthy, and the child might have had more specialised care. This taunt was cruelly unfair, because from the day of her birth, Lowell had made certain that Bianca had everything it was possible for her to have.

In the course of time, the stormy marriage was blessed by a second child, Luke, mercifully whole and strong. Soon after, Lowell qualified as a doctor.

'Good,' Rita told him. 'You've done it, you've got it out of your system — now forget it and do what you were born to do.'

'But — you couldn't forget it?' I ventured to prompt him. He had been so long silent that I feared I wouldn't hear the rest of the story. And I had to hear it. There were things I had to know.

He said abruptly, 'After holding Bianca Maria in my arms — then watching her die? I knew what I had to do. Even before Bianca, I knew.'

'Yes, I can understand that. I really can,' I whispered.

'Rita didn't, unfortunately. She never wanted to see much beyond a First Night at the Met — hoards of Press photographers — some new sapphires to match her eyes . . . ' His voice was so hard that I scarcely recognised it. 'So we had our last battle. I wouldn't surrender, so she had her revenge by pushing me down a flight of stairs. Oh, it was looked on as an accident, of course. I knew better, I knew she'd tripped me deliberately. I nearly died, but I wasn't going to give her that satisfaction . . . '

I shivered with horror at the bitterness I had uncovered. I wondered if the continual effort to crush it down accounted for the harshness in his character that had so disturbed me.

'Lowell, that's a terrible accusation. Perhaps she did want you out of her life — but that doesn't mean she'd try to commit murder,' I protested.

'Well.' He shrugged his shoulders. 'Either way, the result was the same. A few top medics swore I'd never walk again, but I intend to prove them wrong.'

I nodded. Since my first evening here, I had glimpsed him again more than once struggling around the garden in the evening by dint of fierce determination and labouring crutches. Each time I had wanted to run to his aid. I had suffered with him.

For another long moment now he didn't speak, his eyes screwed up in the sunlight, the breeze lifting the curly dark hair on his forehead where pain had etched its mark. Then he lifted his head abruptly.

'We finally separated. Rita took Luke out to the Moroni villa to live — of course, she and the old man both condemn me bitterly for having loused up the family and they've taught Luke to feel the same way. They're just hoping and praying the poor little guy has inherited The Voice! I went back to my mother's place. That diner is her family's business, and she runs it. I was in and out of hospitals for various operations, and between times I helped Ma out in the cafe.

'My mother is an angel incarnate, bless her heart. She just soaked up all my foul tempers and frustrations — until one day this little crippled child came into the cafe. She couldn't hold a spoon or a cup. I fed her while her folks were eating. She was just the age my Bianca would have been — and after they all left, I went outside and cried. It was like coming out of a dark pit. That was the day the first Haven was born.'

His voice shook when he spoke of his little dead child. I knew now that this so dynamic and demanding man was full of a pain unhealed and unhealing.

I couldn't explain to him how strangely stricken I was to know he had a wife and child, something I had never for a moment expected. I just said softly, 'Thank you for telling me. I promise I won't broadcast it around.'

'No, don't broadcast it.' The bitterness crept into his voice again. 'It doesn't say much for my attempts to solve other people's problems when my own life has been such an unholy disaster, does it?'

There had been occasions in the short while I had known him when the depth of his understanding had hauled me back from engulfing despair. I sensed now that our roles were reversed. Somehow I had to find the right words of comfort.

'Lowell, listen to me,' I said softly. This was the second time in these few moments his first name had come naturally to my lips. My hand sought one of his, clenched tightly on the arm of his chair, loosened it, and held it fast. 'Don't ever feel you're not succeeding, don't ever feel you have to give up. All those troubles in your life have made this place possible, don't you see that? They've given you this wonderful goal, they made you what you are — and that's something very, very special.'

As though jolted back to the present, he quickly freed his hand.

'Kind of you to say so. Sorry about the maudlin reminiscences, you should have stopped me. Now, I have work to do. I can't waste any more time out here.'

The chair hummed off towards the house at full power. There was no hint of the tragedy hidden behind his commanding glance or his warm smile. He wouldn't accept help or sympathy or pity. He was far sterner and harsher with himself than he ever was with any of his patients.

I looked after him, wishing he had stayed longer, wishing he hadn't rejected my tentative hand. Clearly, I knew now what I wanted and longed to do. I wanted to hold him in my arms, just the two of us safe and near. To go on holding him until his pain and my pain could merge and melt away.

★   ★   ★

It was on the very next morning that the Saturday post brought a letter from Penny. Six scribbled pages transported me back home to London — for home it still was, suddenly more than ever.

I miss you so much, she wrote. *I shall nag Kevin till he brings me down on the bike for a week-end. Let us know when we can come, won't you? Give Jeremy a big kiss from his Auntie.*

I pictured her so plainly, her tail of bright hair bouncing, her quick, lively step. But, much as I longed to see her, a week-end invitation simply wouldn't do. The children's troubles would upset her, probably Lowell would upset her, too, and, of course, she would tell me I looked worn out and I should come straight home. I just had too much to hide from her, too many problems, too many secrets. I would have to ring or write and find some excuse.

The rest of my mail wasn't much more soothing. A note from Hugh, one of his kind, concerned notes as regular as his phone calls: and also another letter from his aunt, Miss Egerton. Doubtless on his say-so, she enclosed a photo of her little country retreat, all old mellow beams, whitened walls and climbing roses. She told me Hugh had explained all about me and my little boy and she looked forward to welcoming us very soon. *The house is so empty and we can all take care of each other, my dear.*

Hugh didn't miss a trick, I thought, a little cynically. How could anyone with any decency or gratitude say, 'No thanks,' to the lonely old lady?

I screwed up the letters in my pocket as though hoping they would just go away. I was just too tired to solve any of these problems. Weariness was a heavy weight upon me and last night yet again had been tormented by dreams — as though in sleep my mind knew the seashore wasn't far from my bedroom window.

Not once had I dared to go near the beach again since that one solitary time when the sight and sound of the sea had so overwhelmed me. Part of me longed to go, part of me shrank in panic from the very thought.

At breakfast today I had confessed as much to Lowell. It had been unnerving, after yesterday, to see him there surrounded by the excited 'wolves' and 'lions' fresh from their early games practice. I knew my face flushed hotly, but he treated me in business-like fashion, quite off-handedly.

He was rounding up tardy entrants to his Prettiest Seashell competition. When he scrawled my name in as a helper, I begged in an urgent whisper, 'Please, cross me off.'

'For what reason?'

'You know why! The sea, that's why! I — I just couldn't stand it . . . '

His dark eyes were devoid of sympathy. 'Come on, that's not a positive attitude. You won't cure anything by hiding it away. We're going to The Maiden's Pool, so I'll need a lot of supervisors.'

The children went on chattering, the

aroma of scorched toast drifted around me — and my name stayed on the list. Now The Maiden's Pool would be a new dread hanging over my head added to all the others. There were times, like this moment, when Lowell made me so angry I wished him a million miles away; yet still I kept watching him across the room, still straining to hear his voice, longing to glimpse his warm smile — because I was falling in love with him. The truth was impossible to avoid. A deep love, a secret love, a hopeless love. One that surely could only bring more pain to me and to him if ever he should discover it . . .

Oh, indeed, I loved him. And yesterday I had almost let him see how much. Now I knew the story of his tragic life, I yearned too to comfort that secret unsuspected Lowell the world never saw, the man so vulnerable, so hurt.

Or was this all another delusion of my muddled mind? Was I capable of truly loving anyone at all while that obsessive presence of my dead husband, Robert, forgotten and yet unforgettable, haunted my days and tormented my nights?

'Penny for them, Paula.' A concerned Mrs Becker was leaning over to squeeze my arm. 'Are you feeling poorly? Not another headache?'

I felt my face flame again at the mere idea of her guessing my thoughts. Breakfast was over and I had eaten none. Nor had Bridget, or Jeremy, both hunched gloomily in their chairs. Morgan had eaten far too much, his pasty full-moon face still bulging with a huge mouthful. It was well Lowell hadn't especially noticed our table.

Luckily, attention was diverted now, as the tables were being cleared, by the voice of Mrs Burns above the rattle of her trolley.

'Another birthday, Dr Moroni? Another cake? Do you really think I can do all my other work and keep on turning out fancy cakes like a production line?'

'But every one is so good,' he assured her. 'A work of art, Mrs B. And we can't deprive Sarah of her turn. Nine candles, please. Ready by six o'clock.'

'Well, it's a good job I'm just working out my notice here.' She turned fiercely on the helpers whose bad luck had landed them on her rota today. 'You with the freckles, just wipe the tables, don't flood them! Liz Jessop, will you stop gossiping and bring me those plates?'

Lowell was already whirring serenely away. At the door, I saw him glance at Faye Prescott and wink. I wished very much I hadn't seen that wink.

★   ★   ★

Later, a cheery blaze of sunshine found me in charge of a path-sweeping gang. We toiled under a blue, breezy sky. Or at least, we were supposed to toil. In fact, I was giving little attention to this duty.

Anyway, as Sarah was the birthday

girl, surely there was no harm in letting her sit in the sun and watch. Likewise in letting Angela and Eddie sit with her for company. As for Ben, with his steel-supported leg that always held out for baseball, but gave great trouble when work was on hand — it seemed unfair to let him go on sweeping and limping alone.

So it was quite a bevy of lethargic sunbathers that Lowell saw as he approached us suddenly from the house. Too late, Eddie grabbed a broom and raised a cloud of dust, leaves, and sweet-wrappers.

I saw Lowell's face was black as thunder. 'Sure you guys don't want deck-chairs and a round of orange juice?' he asked. But his annoyance wasn't for this alone. 'Telephone for you, Nurse Hastings. Again,' he added curtly.

'For me? Oh, sorry,' I apologised in confusion.

'Well, run along. I'll take over here. And you might tell your famous friend we do have working hours here sometimes — and will you also advise him to mind his own business?'

Not daring to imagine what the two might just have said to one another, I fled up the driveway.

'Paula,' Hugh's velvet-soft voice said. 'How are you? You sound out of breath.'

I explained I had run in from the garden. His next question was less easy.

'Did you hear from Aunt Grace?'

'Yes, and it was a very sweet letter. I haven't had a chance yet to reply.'

'Never mind. I'll pass it on to her. How soon can I say you'll be arriving?'

I began stammering that I wasn't sure if I would be arriving, that maybe we could arrange a holiday visit. In the midst of it. I had to blurt out, 'Please, whatever did you say just now to upset Dr Moroni so much?'

'Was he upset?' Hugh didn't sound displeased. 'I just asked some questions that need straight answers. I've been delving more deeply into the subject of your friend and his Haven clinics. You know the first one folded quite suddenly — but did you also know a child nearly died as a result of being there?'

'Hugh, I don't believe it! Where did you hear . . . ?'

'I have my sources. Reliable sources. As for the financial aspect, I'm afraid there's evidence that Lowell Moroni used donations for that Haven for his own personal use. You remember how uneasy he was when I brought up the subject of money and tried to find out if his grandfather helped with the funds?'

'Hugh, I'm not going to listen,' I told him. 'It's just a horrible pack of lies. Oh, he's not an easy man. Sometimes he drives us all mad, but if you knew him as well as I do, you'd never believe such things! If something happened to a patient it wasn't his fault. And the money — that must have been a misunderstanding.' In full flood, I was struck by another quite appalling thought. 'You're not taking all this any further? You're not starting one of your

TV investigations?'

'Don't you think I should? For the sake of the sick children in his care, Paula, and the parents who've entrusted them to him?'

'Please.' I was nearly sobbing.

This was becoming as unreal as all the rest of my nightmare fantasies. I heard Hugh's voice going on and scarcely made sense of it. Nothing was my fault, he kept saying, but after my illness my judgment was impaired — and that was why Lowell had this strong influence on me. Without question, I needed looking after. He would tell Aunt Grace to expect me soon, and the first chance he had to come down to Cornwall he would collect me — and Dr Moroni could make any objections to Hugh personally!

''Bye for now, Paula darling,' he ended gently. Then the line was dead.

For a long moment I went on standing there. I was still dazed, my head throbbing.

'Are you all right?' an unexpected

voice asked behind me.

Faye Prescott was kitted out in a pale-mint tracksuit, a tennis racquet under one arm. With her were a motley group of children in shorts and T-shirts, including a muffled-up Morgan, a moist-eyed Bridget — and Jeremy sulking along in the rear, which said much for Faye's powers of discipline.

'You all go on ahead,' she ordered them, 'I'll be along in a moment!' Then turned back to ask me, 'Can I do anything to help, Paula?'

I was surprised at her concern. Although from the outset she had always offered help, I had mostly avoided her patronising overtures. I wasn't at all sure I liked Faye. Still less did I like the confidential closeness she had to Lowell which I had glimpsed once or twice.

I said awkwardly that I'd had a misunderstanding with Hugh on the telephone.

'Ah. They happen in the best regulated circles. I've been meaning to ask you, is he planning to give us an airing on his TV show?'

How little she knew how near she was to the truth — and the kind of showing The Haven was likely to get!

'I — I don't know yet, he is quite interested in The Haven . . . ' I stopped and drew breath. She was the last person I would have imagined myself talking to — but at this moment I was upset enough to bury my pride, and those pangs of jealousy along with it. 'Have you known Lowell very long?' I blurted out.

'No, it just seems that way. That's what he does to you! I gave up a good post at a boarding school in Sussex to work here. It started when I heard Lowell give a fund-raising lecture — I thought the project was interesting so I went round to see him afterwards with some questions. Well, he's very persuasive, haven't you noticed?'

I nodded, fervently.

But this surprisingly human and

earnest Faye had more to say. 'He's also rather a wonderful person. However hard he works his staff and his patients, he works himself ten times harder — with a physical handicap that would daunt anyone else. And — he sings like an angel, did you know that?'

'Yes, I do know,' I answered quietly.

Her blue eyes held a dreamy expression. 'You'd think, wouldn't you, that he'd settle for sitting in the sun by the Moroni villa in Capri or wherever, and doing just a few recordings and concerts?'

The plea was quite wistful. It was easy to see Faye would cheerfully settle for sitting in the sun along with him. I wondered, did she have any idea — or did she care — that Lowell had an estranged wife and a child?

The unexpected chat ended abruptly. Both of us heard Lowell's approach. Faye whispered, 'I'm off — if he finds us not giving him his one hundred per cent effort, heads will roll!'

Just as anxious to keep mine on my

shoulders, I fled, too. At this moment, I couldn't face Lowell. I wasn't sure I would ever be able to face him again.

Late in the afternoon, the dining-room had been made festive with coloured balloons. In pride of place stood Sarah's cake, topped splendidly with pink icing and candles, but suffering an unfortunate list to star-board. As I slipped in at the last moment, Lowell was teasing Mrs Burns about her latest creation.

'Did you use the cantilever principle, Mrs B? Or did you borrow the blue-prints from the Leaning Tower of Pisa?' He waved a soothing hand to stem her bristles of protest. 'Never mind, you have yourself a ball — sit down right there ready for the first slice.'

As a flushed and giggling Sarah came forward he gave a signal and the other children blasted forth with gusto: 'Happy Birthday dear Sarah, Happy Birthday tooo yooo . . .'

Momentarily, I was startled to hear Lowell's beautiful liquid voice soar effortlessly into the lead.

While the children took their places, with the usual jostling of plastic chairs, I was busy helping Tony, who was having one of his bad days. Just as I got him settled, Sophie came in, breathless and excited.

'They are not anywhere. I look in ze bedrooms, ze 'obbies-room, ze garden . . . '

'OK, simmer down. Who aren't anywhere?' Lowell prompted.

It was at this instant that I turned to my own table — and found three empty chairs. Sophie was jabbering on that Morgan, Bridget, and Jeremy were nowhere to be found — but on Jeremy's bed she had just discovered a note, addressed to me. My face burning in the sudden glare of attention, I took the paper from her.

I had forgotten Jeremy. I had forgotten him!

'Well?' I heard Lowell demand.

I didn't look at him, nor hand him the sketchy message. Jeremy had gone home to Auntie Penny. He had taken Morgan and Bridget along because they hated The Haven, too. I had forgotten Jeremy — and forgotten too, or ignored, his suspicious interest in the bus-route that connected with London-bound trains.

Still I didn't look at Lowell as I struggled to answer him. 'They've run away. I did know it might happen, and I never told you! Lowell, they're trying to get to my sister in London. Oh, what are we going to do?'

'No, you didn't trouble to tell me about all that, did you?'

There was no explosion of anger. I almost wished there had been, instead of the unnatural quiet of that response. With the room buzzing with excitement all around me, I lifted at last stricken eyes from the paper trembling in my hand.

Lowell's face was darker than I had ever seen it. God forbid, I prayed wildly, that any harm should come to those three forlorn fugitives — but if it did, I would never forgive myself. And nor, I knew, would Lowell ever forgive me!

5

All around me The Haven quaked with excitement. There were exhaustive searches of the premises — seeming pointless to me, but it was just possible Jeremy's note could be a ruse to divert pursuers. Telephone calls buzzed hither and thither. Finally, the yellow mini-bus coughed urgently to life as Mr Burns brought it round to the main door.

I wasn't really much help to anyone. All I could see was a vision of Jeremy's small, defiant face, and Bridget's copious tears, and the mute misery of poor, roly-poly Morgan.

I had let him down, the tragically comical child whose trust I had tried to gain. I had let Jeremy down by not saving him from himself. And Bridget. And Lowell.

It was established the trio couldn't have left long ago, as all three had figured in Faye's afternoon tennis session. Also, they had money for their journey. On Lowell's instructions, I'd checked my handbag, and was shocked to find it had been raided. More than ever, my own son was a complete stranger to me.

Lowell nodded when I confessed the loss. If he would be kind to me, I thought desperately, maybe I could bear this agony of suspense better. But how could I expect him to be kind? It wasn't the children alone who were in jeopardy, but the reputation of his beloved Haven as well. If this became public knowledge, there would be no need to fret over Hugh possibly doing the place harm . . .

'I'm coming with you!' I cried, when I saw him on his way out to the bus. He was leaving Faye completely in charge at this end, especially the telephone contact with the local police, with likely railway stations, and my sister, Penny, in London. At present Penny wasn't answering, so doubtless she and Kevin were blissfully abroad somewhere on his motor-bike and wouldn't return for hours . . .

As Mr Burns was nervously adjusting the special ramp that allowed wheelchair access at the rear of the bus, Lowell glanced round at me. 'Come on, then!'

'Thank you,' I whispered. I clambered in. Before the doors were shut, Mrs Burns came hurrying out of the house with a sandwich-box and a flask.

'Not that those 'young devils deserve it, they need putting across someone's knee! But — they might be half-starved by now.'

'Bless your heart, Mrs B,' Lowell said.

In the bus, too, were Debbie and a local girl on the domestic staff, Jenny Pruett. When we reached the village, Debbie jumped out and ran to the bus shelter, while Jenny went into an adjoining sweet-shop which was still open. The two girls came back after a few moments. There was no need to ask if they had been successful.

Lowell told Jenny to go on asking around, and Debbie hopped back aboard. Mr Burns took the road to Penvor, scene of our weekly Saturday shopping trips. Several times Debbie whispered, 'Don't worry, it'll be all right!'

Both of us were peering at the road, at every wall, gate, and empty spread of grass, longing to see three weary plodding figures.

'Maybe they're hitch-hiking,' Debbie suggested. I had been trying not to think about that. Most passing drivers would be kind to the children, perhaps would even report seeing them — but as well there were such horrific tales in the news these days about kidnappers and molesters. Probably seeing the look on my face, Debbie added, 'But, of course, your Jeremy has been taught not to accept lifts from strangers, hasn't he?'

'I — I don't know,' I had to admit.

It wasn't surprising that she gave me,

his mother, a peculiar look.

The evening had now turned dull and chilly — unless the shivering cold I felt was mine alone. Mr Burns, whose sedate speedometer rarely topped 35, was hurrying along, but still the familiar ride seemed to take for ever.

At Penvor there were lights in a few shops, especially the cafes and gift-shops around the Old Priory. It looked very quiet, very ordinary, callously unmoved by the drama that was going on. At the railway station, Lowell inquired personally. No sign yet of the runaways, he was told. The police were in contact with other stations along the line. They had descriptions. A red-haired boy, a plump boy probably in several coats, and a frail little girl. They couldn't easily be missed.

'But they must be on a train by now, they left hours ago,' I said.

'Sorry, miss,' the stolid booking-clerk repeated, 'we just haven't seen them.'

'But you must have! They can't have vanished into thin air! They had some money, and someone must have sold them tickets — or let them slip through without . . . '

'They didn't get any tickets from here,' the man repeated more tartly. It was Lowell who steered me firmly away from the station and my tirade against the long-suffering clerk. I was almost crying by now with helpless anger, frustration and fear.

Lowell sent me with Debbie to the bus depot, while he went to the police and Joe Burns cruised around the streets. The nightmare went on and on. The people at the bus depot were sympathetic, but no real help. As the streets darkened still more, I wondered what Penny would say when she heard about this — and what the families of Bridget and Morgan would say.

From the bus depot we telephoned The Haven. Faye had no news. Our short dragging walk back to the railway station was like a marathon. Debbie's cheery brightness had dwindled away.

'There's Dr Moroni waving to us!'

she cried out suddenly. 'Quick, Paula, run!'

I ran. I felt her hand clinging to mine. I felt my heart pounding.

The children had turned up at Redbourne, a town farther up the line. They were being kept there for collection.

I couldn't take in any more. Still sick and dazed, I scrambled on to the bus.

★　★　★

The miles to Redbourne seemed endless. Gazing out at the hurrying darkness, I still couldn't believe that when we arrived the three children would be awaiting us, safe and sound.

And yet, they were.

Waiting as well, when we finally reached the lighted old-fashioned station in this fair-sized town, was a police car. Another was just driving away. Inside the station manager's office we found the runaways huddled on chairs, being sustained with hot drinks and snacks — along with a quiet admonitory lecture from a grave-faced police sergeant.

Though so much in my life was forgotten, this scene I would never forget. The merciful relief, the horrific shadow of what might have been . . . And the policeman's voice explaining that ringleader Jeremy's crafty plan was to journey here by two or three small innocent bus rides and their own scuffed feet, then hopefully slip aboard the night train. The daze of unreality holding me collapsed suddenly like a pierced balloon. I could have shaken Jeremy till his teeth rattled in his rebellious copper-coloured head.

'Did you think it was clever, leading us a dance like this? Didn't you realise we'd be almost out of our minds?' I blazed at him. 'Oh, how could you, Jeremy! And dragging the others along with you and getting them all into this trouble, too!'

The boy's grey eyes opened wider at

that onslaught. He muttered defensively, 'I left a note, didn't I?' That was all the response I could get.

'Later, Paula, OK?' I heard Lowell advise me. I didn't want to leave it till later, but there seemed no other way. Morgan, his pasty full-moon face ashen-pale, was trying to disappear inside his numerous pullovers. Bridget, awash with tears, was sobbing out, 'We never meant any harm — we just wanted to stay with Jeremy's aunty, 'cos — 'cos he says she's nice and wouldn't make us feed any rabbits.'

That pitiful mention of the dreaded Tubby and Cuddles damped my anger down as rapidly as it had flared up. That, and the heap of luggage I had just spotted on the floor. Morgan's bulky plastic carrier was stuffed with more woollies and scarves: Bridget's shiny red shoulder-bag gaped open on the handle of a hairbrush. Jeremy, whose mind clearly ran on lines less mundane, had a football and his Space Zoomer kite.

I could imagine him, the moment he arrived at Penny's flat, haring upstairs to show it off to his bosom crony, Adam.

Only now, he wouldn't arrive there. Instead, there would be a ride back to The Haven to face questions and punishments. For Morgan, a return to the daily silent search for a corner to hide in. For Bridget, too many home-sick tears, too many tasks for her crippled hands — and her name on the pet-feeding rota again next week . . .

'The sooner we get them into their beds, the better,' Lowell was saying. 'Of course, I'll check them over thoroughly. But there wouldn't seem to be much physical damage, thank the Lord.' All this while he had been composedly asking and answering questions with the police officers, thanking the railway staff for their kindness — as always, fully master of the situation.

These three children were posing some problems, he admitted with that disarming frankness of his: one who wasn't a patient but did have family troubles, the other two who were newcomers and hadn't yet settled. If there were any negligence, any complaints to be made, he took full responsibility.

It was all over quite quickly. We were soon trooping outside in the chill night air to the mini-bus.

Bridget slept on the way back, huddled in the circle of my arm. Jeremy sat defiantly on his own, wide awake. But it was Morgan who needed most attention. He wasn't built for lengthy hikes culminating in too many gulped-down crisps and biscuits. Sick and ill, his owl-like glasses at half-mast, he was lying on the back seat, obviously tortured by anxious remorse as well as physical symptoms.

'You won't tell my mother, will you?' he asked. 'She'll die if she knows.'

'Everything will be fine, old buddy.' Lowell's hand smoothing back the boy's tangled hair was as kind and gentle as any woman's. 'You've had a rough time. But now you needn't worry about a thing.'

I watched with a strange ache of longing, almost as though by looking and listening I could apply that tender touch and whispered consolation to myself. I needed forgiveness and comfort just now. From the depth of my soul I needed it.

Soon after, Morgan succumbed to attacks of violent nausea, Lowell attended and reassured the unhappy sufferer, with infinite patience, all the way back.

When we reached the dark bulk of The Haven, lights were shining at windows and excited faces were peering down. In a moment the front door was open. There were welcoming voices, ready helping hands. Faye Prescott, in some uncanny way looking elegant at three o'clock in the morning, was authoritatively in charge. She soon had Camilla and Sarah, who greeted us on the doorstep, trailing back reluctantly to their beds.

'Cor, back already, you lot?' Tony called to Jeremy from the landing. 'I told you it wouldn't work if you wouldn't let me go along, too!'

Jeremy glared at him, weary and humiliated. Geoff wanted to know from the stairs, 'When the police caught you, did they have flashing lights and sirens?'

Faye stated quietly that anyone still out of bed in five minutes would face one of her special maths tests after morning class. The threat worked like magic.

I shepherded Jeremy upstairs, and tried to make him comfortable. Clearly this wasn't the time either for explanations or reproofs. Huddled in bed, his clothes in a heap on the floor, he pulled the covers right over his head. Sorry for him, angry with him, miles away from him, I searched for the right words and failed to find them.

Downstairs, order had been restored. Bridget was safely in bed, Morgan was in the sick-room and Mrs Beecher was with him. There was nothing I could do, Faye assured me, I had better just lie down before I fell down.

I heard her actually saying much the same to Lowell — except that in his case she added a lingering hand on his shoulder, her head bent very close to his. 'You look like a ghost, Lowell. I told you I'd look after everything — why don't you just get some rest?'

She was right about the way he looked. His face was grey with fatigue. But he cut her short quite sharply. 'Thanks, I'm grateful for all your help tonight — but when I'm no longer capable of doing my job I'll be the first to let you know!'

Faye bit her lip at that unkind rebuff. Obviously she was fighting an uphill battle.

I could almost have felt some sympathy for her — if I had any emotion to spare. Just now I hadn't.

★   ★   ★

In my neglected bed, sleep came only in broken snatches. My head was too full of dreams and voices. At last I realised I was wide awake, an opaline dawn was touching my window — and the noises were still there. A fragment of a child's cry, a door closing somewhere below.

I bundled on my dressing-gown.

It was Bridget, it seemed, who was in trouble. Still exhausted and terrified after her adventures, she had wandered from her bed half-asleep. I was just in time to find Lowell soothing her as tenderly as he had comforted poor Morgan.

'Come on, honey. You're safe, no need to worry. How about riding back to bed?' From his chair he reached out strong arms to scoop the child on to his knee. 'I don't do this for everyone, but you're special! This button here will get us rolling.'

She gazed at him, fearful and disbelieving. 'I can't press buttons and work things.'

'But you can, Bridget. Can't she,

Nurse Hastings?' he appealed to me, before I realised he was aware of my presence.

He was guiding her stiffened hand firmly towards his control panel. In a moment, the two of them were whirring along the landing. I glimpsed just one tiny flicker of triumph on the child's pale face.

In her bedroom, Camilla and Julie both were slumbering in their corners. I slipped in to arrange the tumbled empty bed before Lowell half-lifted, half-slid her neatly on to it.

'There you go. Are you warm now?'

'Ye-es. I — I thought you'd be ever so cross 'cos we ran away . . . '

'My poor little girl. No, I'm just very sorry you wanted to leave us. Don't you know we'd all miss you a lot? Especially Tubby and Cuddles, they told me so.'

'They didn't,' she said, eyes wide now. 'Did they?'

'Sure they did. Next time you look after them I'll go with you and we'll ask them again. So you won't run off again and leave us all, will you?'

She shook her head solemnly, sudden drowsiness creeping over her like a visible cloak of content. She sighed twice, and slept.

Still Lowell stayed beside her a few minutes longer. Almost absently, dreamily, his hand lingered on her dark hair.

I knew, because I knew the story of his own tempestuous life, that he was living again the brief doomed days of his baby daughter. It was Bianca Maria whom he quietened to sleep, it was Bianca's little lost hand his memory held across the lonely longing years.

When we left Bridget peacefully sleeping, I hardly knew what to say.

'You should have called me to come. I'd have looked after her,' I stammered awkwardly.

He shrugged. 'Sophie was on call. But she was exhausted, poor kid.'

If anyone had a right to exhaustion, he had. But another fear was obsessing my mind. 'Is it because you don't trust me with the children any more? Oh, I don't blame you if you're going to send me home and get someone new for my job — '

'Did I say any of that? Look, why don't you just get some sleep?'

'I can't sleep, I've been thinking and thinking. If Robert — my husband — knew how I'd neglected Jeremy, whatever would he think of me?'

Lowell sighed. 'You don't even remember the guy, so why worry about that? All right, if you can't sleep, go down to the kitchen and make some coffee. I could use some.'

I agreed. I was glad to perform some task, any task.

It was strange to invade Mrs Burns' spotless domain to boil up the kettle at five in the morning. I was just setting out two mugs when Lowell joined me, having come down via the lift. I didn't dare intervene in his minor battle with the kitchen's swing door.

I was aware this was the first time we had really been alone for some while, perhaps even since that unforgettable morning in the garden.

'There's something I have to say. I know it's a lot to ask, but — even if I'm leaving The Haven, tell me you forgive me for yesterday,' I said quietly.

He answered a little absently, 'Sure. You're forgiven.'

'Do you mean that? I shan't ever forgive myself. But — if you let me stay . . . '

'I mean it. And, yes, you can stay. Who am I not to forgive?'

This time his dark eyes lifted to mine, tired, still desperately sad. Perhaps there was something about the hour, the troubles we had just been through together that nerved me actually to mention the forbidden subject.

'Thank you, and can I ask you one more thing? It's not for myself, it's for you. I know you'll be furious and tell me to mind my own business.' I ignored the growing sternness in his face. 'I know you're very unhappy, and I've thought a lot about all you told me about your family troubles, and I believe you should make up the quarrel with your grandfather. At least you could try. He's an old man, Lowell. He can't have so many years left to waste on quarrels.'

'Uh-huh. Opinion noted.' He frowned across at me. 'Is that all?'

'No, it's not all! I was watching you just now with Bridget, and I saw you were thinking about poor little Bianca. But — even though you lost her, you still have a child,' I plunged on clumsily. 'Your son Luke, I honestly think you need him — and I'm sure he needs you just as much. It doesn't matter if you're almost strangers, you could go to see him, or send for him to come here. It's not too late.'

I stopped there, partly for breath, partly because of the blaze in his black eyes. I had known him so short a time, in many ways I didn't know him at all — but his torturing memories and his loneliness were abiding pain to me.

'Well now, that's a very pretty speech, but aren't you forgetting just one thing? Look at me, take a good look!' he invited harshly. 'Yes, a boy needs a father — but he sure as hell doesn't need a guy in a wheelchair to play nursemaid to, and pity, and despise!'

A violent gesture sent his coffee mug tumbling and splashing to the floor. He made a vain attempt to retrieve it, and painfully straightened up, his forehead flushed and damp with the effort.

'Does that convince you?' he demanded fiercely. 'Luke has a good home, a good life, he's better off without me. Anyone but a complete fool can see that!'

'Then I'm a complete fool, because I can't see it!' My own voice rose suddenly with a passion to match his. 'But I see something else — that you're an out and out hypocrite, Lowell Moroni, do you know that? 'Think positive, act positive, never accept defeat' you keep on bullying and badgering into all these poor little

Haven kids — and I really thought you believed it and set them a wonderful example. But now, I'm not sure you believe any of it, not when you don't practise a single word you preach. It wouldn't hurt Luke to have a 'guy in a wheelchair' for a father — but he is better off without a pretender with double standards!'

There were tears flooding my eyes, tears of anger and pain. I turned blindly away and fled, back towards the quiet of my room, safely away from him. I wanted to go on shouting at him. I wanted to take him in my arms and hold him close to my aching heart, to find comfort in comforting him. He was no saint, for all his dedication to his chosen work; his great strength had its flaws and weakness . . . And I loved him, I loved him. Lowell — so human and vulnerable and proud and alone . . .

He and I together, I thought as I tumbled back on to my rumpled bed, both of us were victims of our own dangerous obsessions. Me with a past I couldn't remember. He with a past he couldn't forget.

★   ★   ★

It took The Haven a day or two to settle itself back to normality. For me, it needed longer. Still I was haunted constantly by the knowledge of how much worse the children's escapade could have turned out. Still I was burdened by remorse, the certainty that I could well have prevented the whole thing from happening.

The only possible way to make amends was to concentrate totally on my work. I volunteered for extra hours and duties, I strove to prove to Lowell that his continued trust in me wasn't misplaced.

The other very difficult problem facing me was how to get through to Jeremy. He was so clearly in need of more love and understanding than he was getting from me. His grief for his dead father was healing with time, with the daily unfolding of his young life — which was just as it should be, but his second loss, the mother who looked the same and yet wasn't at all the same, was so much more complicated and slower to find any healing.

Lowell had had a long talk with him about running away and causing me so much worry, about involving two other children, about rifling my handbag, and all the rest of it: none of the trio were being specifically punished, but Lowell made it clear to them he expected improved behaviour and improved progress. I tried quite desperately to find the right moment for a heart-to-heart chat with Jeremy that would bring us closer. But either I bungled my attempts hopelessly or that right moment didn't come.

As well, of course, there was my continuing problem of Hugh — whose work had taken him north this week filming a holiday scheme for elderly disabled which he was launching. I was glad he was safely out of the way, one anxiety I could shelve.

Indeed, probably as an aftermath of all the nervous strain of these past days, sudden anger erupted in me when I considered how he was trying to run my life and move me around like a pawn. He had saved my life, he had showered me with kindness and offered me a future that would be a whole new world — but I was still entitled to a will of my own, my own feelings and my own opinions.

Impulsively, I sent him a note, pointing out that, despite my illness, I was not a child, not incapable, and I would be pleased to visit his Aunt Grace when I was ready, which wasn't just yet! Afterwards, half-triumphant, half-regretful, I wasn't at all sure exactly what I had written; only that I certainly steered very clear of the accusations of personal dishonesty and professional ineptitude he had directed at Lowell.

I was trying very hard not to think

about those at all. Hugh wouldn't risk one of his public investigations unless he had some very concrete evidence, so the whole thing just had to be a mistake that would blow over!

Unlike the scheduled visit to The Maiden's Pool, which wasn't blowing over and was very, very imminent.

'Strong shoes, warm anoraks, two o'clock sharp — no dawdlers!' Lowell said at breakfast. I had asked him twice already to let me off, to no avail. As the dining-room emptied, I tried one last ploy, offering to stay behind and look after Morgan.

'No need. Morgan is fit enough to stir himself and come along with us.'

'Oh,' I muttered. Well, perhaps it would rain.

But those dark clouds kept on sailing past without decanting a drop. Punctually, the outward-bound party loaded itself into the mini-bus, the Camera Club bringing their equipment, others provided with sketch pads, notebooks, and binoculars for bird-watching. Everyone had collecting bags for pebbles and shells.

Faye and Lowell between them kept strict order during the drive along the picturesque coastal road.

When Joe Burns parked at the space provided for sightseers, there were 'oohs' and 'aahs' from the party. Indeed, it was a sombre and striking spot, especially under today's lowering skies. A little sheltered cove was separated from us by a mass of rocks and boulders and fell away suddenly to a deep hollow in which shimmered ominously the supposedly bottomless depths of the pool where the luckless maiden of the legend was drowned.

Lowell gave strict instructions that everyone must stick together in groups and no one must explore alone. The path and shallow steps leading down from the road had been provided with a safety rail: but almost at once Camilla Price tripped and fell, and from then onwards I was busy attending to her grazed knee — and Eddie's coughing fit, and Morgan's still queasy stomach — to the exclusion of our very picturesque, very frightening surroundings.

At the foot of the path, the pool had its own strange little beach littered with quaintly coloured pebbles, and the shells of unwary sea creatures that had found their way through unseen rocky tunnels far below. Geoff and Ben speculated that the maiden would have been sucked into a tunnel, too, and stuck halfway. No doubt her whitened bones were still lodged there, picked clean by generations of hungry crabs.

'Goodness gracious, you boys have got horrible, morbid imaginations!' Mrs Beecher exclaimed. 'Why don't you just collect some of those pretty pebbles like the others?'

They even enlivened that tame occupation, pointing dramatically at a reddish-streaked one Bridget had just found, and whispering to her 'Blood!'

Bridget dropped it with a little shriek. A sprinkling of rain was blowing now in the strengthening breeze. The camera people took their shots under Lowell's supervision. How he had descended the path in his chair, and how he would get back up again, I wasn't sure.

'Looks like we chose the wrong day. Ten more minutes, gang!' Lowell informed everyone.

I was vastly relieved. But I didn't get away with it quite so easily.

While everyone packed up, Lowell intended taking some seascape slides for the next evening show, from a viewpoint a little farther along. He waved a casual hand at a steep path curling out of sight. 'I'll need a hand with the camera — so will you come, Paula?' he asked me directly.

'Me? Oh, I'm an awful dunce with photography!'

Faye volunteered at once, looking not at all pleased when he declined. He preferred her to stay with the kids, he said, because we wanted no more drowned maidens. If that was a compliment to her efficiency, she didn't seem to appreciate it.

I was quite sure Lowell could manage his photography unassisted, and this was some prearranged plan to make me face up to my fears. I hung back as long as I could, but the rough path, which looked impossibly dangerous for a wheelchair, decided me. Annoyed, reluctant, afraid, I had to go with him.

'Well done,' he said with approval as I scrambled and slithered along in his wake.

'You're asking for a nasty accident. You've no business coming to these places!'

He turned on me that very disarming smile of his. 'A couple of days ago, weren't you accusing me of not living up to The Haven principles?'

I grumbled on under my breath, stones in my shoes and the wind clawing my hair, longing to get back to the shelter of the bus. But after a few minutes I forgot those trifles. The path took us down through a narrow cleft in the cliffs — and suddenly we were face to face with the wild splendour of the sea.

The sky and the water were iron-grey, the wind here was fierce, robbing me of breath and of thought. I gazed aghast, the vista of stormy shore battering my senses.

Then instinctively I hid my face in cold, shaking hands. But other hands, strong and relentless, roughly pulled away the protecting fingers from my eyes.

'Was it like this? Just like this? Don't drive the memory back, let it in, let it all in!'

'I can't look, don't make me look!'

'Yes, you can! You must! Remember it all, Paula, remember it. The boat, the storm — the faces, the voices in the wind . . . '

I was panting, half-sobbing. But I couldn't escape the dominant will that had transcended mine — and like a shadow on the edge of my mind, half within reach, there came to me a vision of a man . . . A man young, tall, dark-haired, with a thin, thoughtful face, and Jeremy's grey eyes ... Oh, yes, dear heaven, how well I knew those eyes!

I heard my own voice cry out, 'We nearly died! All of us nearly died!'

'That's right, but you didn't die, and Jeremy didn't die — it was Robert who was drowned, Robert and Caroline ... Listen, Paula, can you hear them calling to you?'

I whispered, 'Caroline?' The girl Hugh loved and would have married, the girl who had looked at him with open adoration. Another ghost on the edge of my mind, a laughing, sun-burned face, long, wind-blown hair. 'Yes, you and your family come with us,' she told me far, far back in time. 'We'll have a smashing day — and I'll pack some pills for sea-sickness, just in case.'

But the tossing boat made her hit her head. There was blood on her fright-ened face, a crimson stain mingling with the rain and cascading spray — so how could she struggle for life in the cruel, cold tide that was sweeping her away, that would impale her like a rag doll on the teeth of those lethal, lathered rocks? Yes, I could see her now in the water, the trail of her long, light hair! I cried out, 'Robert! — Caroline's hurt, can't you see? — Robert, we've got to save her!'

Somehow, I was running, stumbling, and splashing over the rough beach towards that ghastly, drowning shape there in the water, the rapier wind slicing my face. We had to be in time, we had to be! Caroline, hold on, hold on, we're coming! Caroline, hold on, you've everything in the world to live for . . .

'Paula, wait for me! Paula, wait till I get this damn thing moving,' a voice shouted behind me. But not Robert's voice, never Robert's. This angry, alien voice, snapped in one shocked instant my bubble-fantasy.

I knew that awesome trail on the water wasn't the hair of a drowning girl, but a garland of weed. I knew the vision of my lost husband was a delusion of light and wind. Following my headlong dash to the sea wasn't Robert Hastings, but another man, quite another — who was struggling furiously to move a powered wheelchair stuck fast on the rocky beach.

'Paula, will you wait for me? Do you hear me?'

He needn't have worried. I was back in the present, in stark reality — just in time to avert a certain accident. Inspired with a strength I didn't know I possessed, I raced back to fling protecting arms around Lowell as his chair tilted crazily.

Somehow he was back on an even keel. I was trembling all over, partly from shock, from the closeness of him in my arms — and partly from all those past memories that had stirred and now again were lost. For lost they were, in the mists veiling my mind. I reached for them now again, and reached in vain.

'Don't be afraid.' Lowell was soothing me softly and insistently. 'It's all over, you've done very, very well. And we've proved the memories are still there. So we'll beat this thing between us. Very soon we'll beat it!'

He was warming my hands in his, his eyes compelling mine, driving away fear and nightmare. When he was kind and gentle like this, I would have gone to the ends of the earth for him. I stood there in the slanting rain, very near to him. My arms that had so briefly held him still ached with their longing.

We still hadn't started back when anxious little Mr Burns arrived in search of us. He had come down from the bus to help with the main party, and Faye had despatched him in our wake. I was glad to see him. The uphill scramble wasn't easy.

By the time we caught up with the others, making a more or less orderly retreat, the rain was a downpour and everyone was drenched.

Back at The Haven I was quickly

engrossed in hot baths for the children, and the steaming bowls of soups which Mrs Burns dispensed along with dire forecasts of pneumonia. Just when I realised I was nearing exhaustion. Lowell told me I was excused all further duties. For me, too, the orders were a hot bath, a hot meal, and early to bed.

Meekly, gladly, I obeyed. When finally I trailed to my attic, I looked in on Jeremy, already asleep in his adjoining room. Under a coppery fire of hair his face on the pillow was thin and serious. I thought suddenly of that bright hair awash with the tossing seaweed, that pale, small face void and senseless dipping beneath the groping tide. So nearly I had lost him, along with all else.

For this moment, he wasn't a stranger. I wanted to clasp him safe and close, the son I had borne and nursed and loved, long ago in another world.

But I didn't wake him. Just gently I kissed his forehead under that blaze of damp hair, and crept away softly to my own bed.

★ ★ ★

'Have you seen this?' Annie Beecher asked me. Just back from the village, she looked upset as she flourished the local weekly newspaper. I heard her prophesying darkly, 'There'll be a big row about it. Oh, Debbie, have you seen it, dear?'

Debbie, awed and round-eyed, evidently had. I changed my mind about going for a walk while the children were in Faye's morning class, and curiously took the paper.

RUNAWAY CHILDREN IN MIDNIGHT CHASE leaped to my eyes in bold black letters, with a photograph of The Haven — looking so dead and deserted that it surely was taken when the occupants were still in their beds. I skimmed through a glowing account of the flight of three young inmates from the controversial Haven Clinic for

Disabled and Disturbed Children, run by American-based Dr Lowell Moroni, grandson of the famous operatic tenor, Guilio Moroni.

Though Dr Moroni was unavailable for comment, from another source close to The Haven they had details of the late-night pursuit of three runaways, so unhappy at the clinic that they had attempted the long journey home to London. The trio were found by the police at Redbourne, cold and hungry, the little girl still clutching her favourite red bag containing her few possessions.

'Good grief,' I muttered.

There was also an editorial, which I read quite aghast. It questioned the need for such a specialised establishment — which was of still wholly unproven success — occupying fine premises which could be the perfect answer for the long-established and deserving St Christopher's Orphanage near Penvor, forced to vacate its present old, overcrowded building shortly and desperately seeking a new home.

Generous purchase offers made by the St Christopher's Administrative Committee for The Haven had all been flatly refused, despite the fact that the clinic occupied only part of its over-spacious site and one whole wing had never been properly renovated or used. And so on, all in a similar strain, all exuding behind-the-scenes insight.

It was my first knowledge of all these undercurrents. But if they weren't yet public knowledge, plainly this was just what was needed to stir them up! I wondered with sudden alarm what Lowell was going to say and do. I wondered, too, who could conceivably be the mysterious source at The Haven responsible for leaking such intimate details so fully?

'Phone for you, Paula — Hugh Egerton all the way from York,' Faye Prescott's voice broke in on me. I gave an almighty start, before remembering that at this hour on Fridays her school-room rang with erratic French Conversation under Sophie's tutelage.

She added, evidently spotting the newspaper in my hand, 'Ah, yes! We're making quite a splash in the local Press this week, aren't we?'

'Aren't we just! I think it's disgraceful,' Annie Beecher exploded. Excitedly she hailed Lowell, just whirring along the landing from the lift. 'Dr Moroni, have you seen The Examiner, because if you haven't you really should.'

He said shortly that he had been too busy to read newspapers. However, he reached out for the offending paper. My hand shook as I gave it to him.

I watched him scan the sensational columns, rapidly, stern-faced. I saw the dark frown, the angry glint in his eyes as he crumpled the sheet and flung it away, right over the banister and down the stair well.

'That,' he said curtly, 'is the best thing to do with that!'

'But — but we can't just ignore it,' Annie quavered. 'Can we?'

'It isn't just nonsense, it's mischievous nonsense. We certainly needn't come unglued over it. We've more useful things to do. OK, folks?'

At that subtle hint, we scattered. For me, that meant a dash down to the telephone, as Hugh had been hanging on for several minutes.

Now, I apologised to him shakily for the delay, and he said it didn't matter.

'Have you read your local newspaper today?'

'Have I read . . . ?' I echoed. Once again I was aghast, unbelieving. 'Yes, I have.

'But how on earth have you seen a Cornish paper when you're in Yorkshire?'

'I have my sources.'

Not more sources! The word stirred me to retort hotly, 'Then I hope they also told you it's a mountain out of a molehill! Lowell called it mischievous nonsense!'

'Did he, indeed? Well, he won't dismiss a filmed investigation quite so easily, I think. I'm working out my schedule to piece together a few interviews. For instance, parents and relatives of your patients — I'm sure they must be worried that this sort of thing can happen.'

'Hugh, you can't do this! I — I won't let you . . . '

'You're very upset, and I'm sorry. I wanted you to be safely away from it all by now and be spared this unpleasantness. But you simply wouldn't listen — and you still won't listen. So, I'm afraid it's my plain duty to carry on.'

'Your duty to break Lowell and ruin all the wonderful work he does?' I flared at him anew. 'Or — or is it because I'd rather stay here with him than marry you?'

'Paula.' He said just my name, in shocked reproach.

'Well, that's what it looks like,' I muttered. 'Hugh, you just don't know him and the things he can do. It's like a gift he has, a special sort of gift. A couple of days ago he almost cured my lost memory — yes, he did. I started remembering everything, Robert and

Caroline, and the sea and the boat
. . . Then I lost it all again, but next
time maybe he'll cure me for keeps!
And he'll cure these children, too, if
he's left alone and not hounded.'

'Paula. Will you just listen to me?'

'No, I won't listen! I trust Lowell,
and I always shall! And if you're setting
out to damage him, you'll damage me,
too, I'm warning you!'

My voice gave out completely. I put
the phone down, without even a
goodbye.

At the foot of the stairs, I stopped to
retrieve a crumpled ball of newspaper.
Its printed words whirled in my head.
Who could have been responsible?
Hugh knew all about it, he was involved
somehow, but how could he have
supplied all those eye-witness details? It
must be someone who knew and saw
The Haven from the inside, who knew
all about local affairs, who had to some
extent penetrated Lowell's confidence.

And that narrowed down the choice
considerably in my confused reckoning,

to one person alone. Absurd, of course, but who fulfilled all those conditions other than Faye Prescott?

Faye, whom Lowell trusted and relied upon. Faye, who so jealously worshipped the ground beneath him.

6

'And so may I ask all of you, as you sit in your homes tonight — these are families, too, give all you can spare before it's too late for them. Post off your donation to the Hugh Egerton New Appeal for African Children . . . '

The voice, velvet-soft, yet filling the room, was movingly earnest. The blue clear eyes looked straight into the eyes and consciences of his listeners. At a plain office desk, he was making his appeal, yet the functional surroundings were luxury compared to the pitiful scenes he had just shown us of ravaged faces and matchstick limbs.

'It does make you think, Paula,' Mrs Beecher said soberly, across the heads of a rather restive Haven audience in the lounge. 'And, my goodness, isn't he a charmer,' she added. Severely then, she shushed Tony, who was demanding,

'Can't we turn off this dull old stuff and switch over to 'Captain Death On The Black Planet'?'

I nodded vaguely at Annie. Whether the channel was changed after Hugh's quiet farewell, I hardly knew. His own personal spell had come over to me so strongly that it possessed me still. Suddenly, it was impossible to believe any of the base motives and malicious intentions I had attributed to this man. He must truly believe he was doing a genuine service in investigating the peculiarities of The Haven, in recommending the health authorities to check up on not just its treatment methods but the integrity of its founder.

Yet, equally, I was still convinced he would use any means in his considerable power to put a stop to my work with the children. He believed it was too taxing for me, and he wanted to remove me from what he called Lowell's 'Svengali influence.' Smashing The Haven would achieve that.

Today was still only the day following

the local newspaper sensation —
though it seemed much longer since I
began all my feverish conjectures about
Hugh's possible involvement and
whether it was too crazy to link Faye
with the affair. But today I had stopped
agonising over who tipped off 'The
Examiner.' I held in my hand Hugh's
latest letter, which had arrived this
morning. He must have posted it very
soon after I'd slammed the phone down
on him yesterday in anger.

He told me I was clearly distraught
on the telephone. He wasn't angry, just
so concerned for you, darling . . . And
if I preferred not to take on the
responsibility of Aunt Grace, he
understood. He would make other
arrangements for the old lady. Maybe
the best answer after all, when I so
obviously needed help myself.

As always, he had a perfect answer.
Could we not simply get married right
away?

*I've found a little place I know
you'll like. We can rent it furnished for*

six months while we look for some-where to buy, he wrote — and as further persuasion he enclosed an estate agent's leaflet, describing Bryony Cottage as *the ideal country retreat to escape from the rat-race,* and providing a photograph of weathered beams and chintzy curtains. In such rustic isolation, Hugh was sure I would get well. He would find a suitable housekeeper so I needn't bother with tiresome chores, and would have company when he was away working.

So, here was all my future life worked out. A quiet private wedding, no fuss and no publicity. The best boarding-school possible for Jeremy, unlimited rest and country air for me. When Hugh's current assignment finished he would come down to see me, he promised, and settle everything the way I wanted it. He added just one little ominous footnote at the bottom of the page: the beginnings of his Haven inquiry were *making good progress.*

I'd carried that letter around with me

all day. I could keep it to myself no longer. With the children glued to their Saturday television ration, I murmured an excuse to Annie and slipped away.

Could I approach Lowell for counsel? If indeed Lowell would still grant it, after the personal insults I'd showered on him recently.

As I went down the corridor, the sound of the television was replaced by an appealing fragment of piano melody. Outside Lowell's room it was clear. My knock went unnoticed, so I peeped inside. Evidently he had just returned from his regular constitutional around the grounds: the garden door stood half-open, the breeze from the sea stirring the curtains. He sat in his wheelchair at the piano, beneath the watchful portrait of his grandfather. I saw his strong square hands moving very sensitively over the keys. Whatever else he did with his life, Lowell had music in his blood.

He turned to me with an inevitable, 'Hi!'

'Oh, please don't stop,' I said quickly, but he had stopped already, spinning his chair away from the piano. 'I know that piece of music, Robert used to — ' I began.

'Yes? What did Robert do?'

'I — I don't know,' I said lamely. 'It just made me think of Robert.'

'You told me he collected records, maybe that Consolation is among them. That's very good.' His brow was still wet from the recent painful effort of movement as he smiled at me, the warm, bright smile that was like a balm. 'Well don't stand over there, come in! You're the person I need, I'm out of my depth here.'

He waved a hand at his desk, more cluttered than ever with books. He was compiling a general knowledge quiz for the children, he explained, including several history questions for Morgan. And two heads were better than one.

'I'll try, but — wouldn't Faye be better?' I demurred.

'Oh, sure, if we needed a very

professional school test for bright kids. I want something that'll give the ordinary little guy a fighting chance.'

Typically Lowell, of course. The Lowell Hugh didn't know, nor want to know. I sat down obediently to thumb through a history book, but it was impossible to concentrate for long.

'I'm sorry, I've got to talk to you and to warn you . . . ' I said suddenly.

As he tossed his pen aside and turned to face me, my heart was racing, from the nearness of him, and from fear of his reactions to what I must say. I stumbled on, 'Yes, warn you about the awful things Hugh is planning to do . . . '

I wasn't quite sure what I said to him. Somehow a jumble of words poured out, that despite all my pleading Hugh was investigating The Haven, raking up anything detrimental to make public — and already he had unearthed some unpleasant rumours about Lowell that would soon need a rebuttal. Then I waited for the violent storm.

But the storm didn't come. From Lowell Moroni such restraint was disturbing.

'Well, much obliged for the warning. But I'd guessed already. If friend Hugh wants a battle, he can have one! When the time comes I'll demand a personal interview, live on camera, and Mr Egerton won't know what's hit him! Begging your pardon,' he added, 'I was forgetting about the likelihood of wedding bells.'

'That's something else I want to say!' Hastily, I dumped in front of him Hugh's letter, complete with the Bryony Cottage details. 'First he wanted me to go and nurse his old aunt who lives miles from anywhere, and — and now there's this!'

'Paula, this is a very personal letter. From him to you.'

'Please read it. Because — I'm running out of answers.'

He took his time, carefully digesting the letter. Then, frowning, deeply serious, his eyes looked straight into mine. 'Tell me something — are you in love with this guy?'

'I — I'm not quite sure,' I evaded. My face was on fire. Supposing he asked next, 'Is there anyone else you care for more?'

'Well, answer me something else. Why is he so anxious to bury you away as though you're infectious?'

This was easier. 'Isn't that obvious? He wants me to get completely well, of course.'

'Uh-huh.'

That routine response radiated disbelief. I looked at him. 'You don't think so? All right, what other reason could there possibly be?'

As luck would have it, I got no further. A tap on the door heralded Sophie's excited presence and fractured English, complaining that zose bad boys insisted on watching Captain Death to the bitter end, regardless of their rota of evening duties.

'They do, do they?' Lowell sighed resignedly and turned towards the door.

He apologised to me over his shoulder. 'Sorry, Paula. Another time, OK?'

I wished very much Sophie had let the boys have their way.

* * *

To be quiet and get completely well. Whatever Lowell's weird private suspicions, that was the only wish Hugh had for me. Only, of course, I had never really accepted it, because it clashed so strongly with my own compulsion to stay at The Haven — where life was never quiet!

And yet, soon after that unfinished talk with Lowell, I did begin wondering whether Hugh's prescription for me had been right all along. Because, all at once, it seemed my half-clouded mind was getting far cloudier.

It was a late-evening phone call from Penny in London that began it.

'Paula, lovely to hear you! You sound fine. Look, will you be terribly upset if I don't accept your invitation this time?

Oh, you know how much I want to see you, only this week-end — well, it's Kevin's birthday, you see — '

The bright voice went bubbling on. I stammered stupidly, 'My invitation?'

'It was sweet of you to ask me, and next time you've a free week-end, of course I'll stay with you and see where you work. But this Saturday we're giving a party — just a few friends and some pizzas and a couple of bottles of plonk — '

My head was whirling in a daze of unreality. Had I really invited Penny for the week-end? Could I actually have invited her then completely forgotten? I tried to say, 'Penny, wait a minute, I don't remember — I can't remember at all — '

'I know,' she sympathised, 'you haven't got your memory back yet, you poor love — but never mind, I think you're wonderful to stick at your job with the kids, you've real guts! Oh, and everyone sends their love — '

She broke off there, because she was

baking Kevin's cake and it smelled, she said, as though it was cremating. She promised to ring next week, then suddenly the line was dead. I stood there for several minutes, just listening to the echoes of her voice.

Was Penny crazy, or was I? Hadn't I definitely decided not to risk inviting her to The Haven, in case the patients upset her susceptible heart, or maybe in case she was too persuasive in cajoling me to return to the London flat?

So, all night I tossed and turned, revolving in my mind the same question — was Penny crazy or was I? In the morning, heavy-eyed, I was nauseated by the sights and scents of breakfast. I let Morgan get away with double portions of everything, his podgy, pale cheeks crammed like a prudent hamster's.

Mrs Burns cornered me while keeping a fierce eye on her table-clearing squad. 'Ah, yes, I've been wanting to see you — about the young girl staying here for the week-end! I really can't provide rooms for relatives,' she told me tartly. 'I've enough to do without running a hotel as well. Can't you book the young lady in at the village somewhere for a couple of nights?'

I stared at her.

'Can't you do that?' she repeated. 'St Owen doesn't have much, but it does have two or three hotels. Have you tried them?'

'No. No, I haven't. Mrs Burns — did I really ask for a room for Penny?'

'Of course you did,' Mrs Burns said sourly. 'What do you think I'm talking about?'

I didn't think. I couldn't think. I backed away, out of the emptying room.

Somehow, I got through the next couple of hours. When the children had their mid-morning break from classes I was on playground duty, my thoughts miles away. In the middle of it, Faye approached, smiling pleasantly.

'Paula, good news! I've just spoken to the garage, they'll definitely fix my car by Friday — so I'll be able to run you to Penvor to meet your sister after all.'

Not again! I almost screamed the words aloud. I was wide awake, the sun warm on my face, and I knew quite clearly what was happening. As though losing all memory of the past wasn't enough, now I was losing touch with the present.

'You look tired,' Faye sympathised. 'I should take it easy.'

When she left me I went about moving in a trance, no longer part of the world around me. Every moment I feared someone else would come up and start telling me about some other unknown arrangements I had made, more of this inescapable delirium, another proof of my disintegrating hold on reality.

'Paula, are you feeling well?' Debbie asked when I went back indoors. Sophie and Jenny, and even some of the children, stared and looked concerned. Lowell wasn't around, I knew he was in Exeter seeing a prospective new patient.

It was Lowell I wanted.

'Look, my dear.' I felt an arm around me. 'Come and lie down a while,' Annie Beecher insisted. 'Let's go up to your room.'

'But I'm supposed to be in the Hobbies Room at twelve o'clock.'

'Nonsense! I'm relieving you of all duties until further notice. I'll take full responsibility if Dr Moroni wants to know.'

I gave in, and let her escort me up to my bedroom, shade the window, and plump up my pillow. To please her, I lay down.

I buried my face in the pillow and mumbled that I would try to sleep. Annie left me, and shortly after sent up some tea. I tossed and turned for maybe an hour longer, my head throbbing. Then Jenny peeped round the door to ask, 'Are you awake? You have a visitor. Mrs Beecher says are you well enough to come down or . . . ?'

It couldn't be Penny! I pushed red-gold strands of hair from my eyes and slid shakily off the bed.

Downstairs, there was amazingly bright sunshine at the windows. The aroma of lunch lingered, but the house was quiet — evidently the children were out of doors. In the hall, my visitor waited. A tall, fair-haired, blue-eyed man, sitting there gazing in turn at a row of children's paintings, and the furry feline shape of Cleopatra pensively guarding the fish-tank.

'Here she is, she wasn't asleep,' Jenny was saying, suddenly all bright eyes and crimson cheeks. Annie, similarly flushed and nervous, amplified, 'But we're all really worried about Paula today, Mr Egerton, she isn't at all well.'

'I can see that. I'm sure you've taken very good care of her, Mrs Beecher,' Hugh's unmistakable voice assured her. Then he turned to me, both hands outstretched. 'Paula, I'm not a ghost, don't look at me like that. Weren't you expecting me?'

'No!' Panic stirred in me anew. Was he going to say I had invited him too?

235

'But I wrote you. Oh, well, never mind all that.' His arm was around me.

He was obviously shocked by the state of me. I knew I must look a creased, crumpled sight, wild-haired and ashen-faced.

I heard Annie fluttering on self-consciously — 'I'm so sorry Doctor Moroni isn't here, he went to see someone — then he was consulting a builder about converting our tower wing into an arts centre or a theatre or some such. Some of our kiddies are in there now, drawing plans on how they'd like to use it.'

'Correction!' Faye Prescott smiled, appearing, as it seemed to me, from nowhere. 'They're busy arguing over Tony's stupendous scheme to use the tower as a beacon to signal mini-submarines bringing in a fortune in smuggled goods. Well, you have to admit, it's original. Lowell always says that child will go far. You know, when Tony first came to us after a car smash, he was a little ghost in a wheelchair. It's a wicked thing to say, but he was much less trouble then than he is now.'

This narrative gave me time to pull myself together just a little. Hugh was listening to her attentively, and she kept on smiling at him with all her usual bright assurance. I even noticed she had on a particularly smart pencil-skirted suit in charcoal-grey.

A moment later, I was annoyed with myself for bothering with such a trifle. I remembered suddenly Hugh's recent letter, the shattering letter I'd showed Lowell, promising to come here soon to settle the cottage and the wedding. That was why he had come! On a day when I was wholly unable to make decisions, when I was living in a dream. If only Lowell were here, I thought desperately.

'We don't expect our chief back till six, maybe seven, the way Joe Burns drives,' Faye was telling Hugh. 'But I'm sure he'd be pleased to know you've come to take Paula out for a drive, right away from The Haven. Maybe the atmosphere here is getting to her. She's still very new, and we do take some getting used to.'

'That's what I had in mind.' Hugh's arm around me tightened gently. 'The car's outside, it's a beautiful afternoon. Do you want to fetch a coat, Paula?'

I didn't want to go. I just couldn't think how to get out of it.

* * *

Indeed, the afternoon was beautiful. Fragments of cotton-wool cloud drifted in a wide blue sweep of sky. As Hugh's car glided down the drive, I was cushioned in soft upholstery and warm sunshine.

He drove quite slowly, not choosing the coast road, but turning away from the sea. He said very little, obviously wanting me to rest and relax without being pestered with questions or advice.

'Have you eaten at all today? Mrs Beecher said you skipped lunch, but you do need to keep up your strength,' he pointed out gently. 'Suppose we stop somewhere for a meal? I'm ravenous, too. I rushed off down here instead of spending the day on mountains of paperwork.'

Mile after smooth mile, we were leaving behind The Haven and all its problems and cross-currents. The ache in my head had eased a little. I settled back more comfortably in my seat and let a welcome peace flow over me. The sunshine lighted up the fresh new greenery of early summer, the grey Cornish villages, the gardens bright with flowers.

'Shall we try this place?' he suggested.

It was a pleasant country inn called The Five Goats. It had tables under some gnarled old apple trees. I didn't really want to stop, but to please him I agreed to sit in the garden and nibble a sandwich.

In fact, the solid food was impossible to swallow, but I was glad of some chilled fruit juice. We had been there only a few minutes when a family of tourists pulled up. I saw one of them nudging the others, and there were the usual whispered comments, 'It is him!'

Hugh murmured to me, 'Caught again.' It ended, of course, with him signing autographs, and saying a few pleasant words. All the while I was horribly conscious of looking a complete mess. It was hardly fair on Hugh to be seen with such an unattractive woman. I abandoned my attempts to eat, longing now only to get back to the security of the car.

When at last we managed to escape, I huddled back thankfully into my seat and tried to apologise. 'I — I'm so sorry — I don't know what everyone must think of me! Only I've had such a bad day. And yesterday too . . .'

'It's all right, never mind what anyone thinks. Just tell me why today was bad. Can't I help?'

'I don't think so. It's just the things that keep happening to me, things I can't understand. Oh, if I tell you, you'll think I'm crazy!'

'Not crazy. Just a little sick. Why not try talking about it? Sometimes just telling someone can help.'

He was very kind. I found myself pouring out, in a muddled rush, those events that had plunged me into a nightmare: Penny's call, Mrs Burns' refusal of the room. Faye's offer of her car.

I saw Hugh fowning.

'I don't know when it might happen again. Hugh, I — I can't go on like this . . .'

His hand was gently stroking my hair. 'It might not happen again.'

'But suppose it does!' I clung fast to that caressing hand.

'You do have a way out. You know that, don't you? You know I'll take care of you. Whenever you want, whenever you're ready.'

I nodded mutely. I could find no more words. I heard him saying, 'Come on, you're shivering. Shall I drive you back now? Do you want to go back to The Haven?'

I wasn't even sure about that, but I nodded again. It was such an incredible relief to be cossetted and comforted. I began to think, perhaps Hugh had been right all along, I had never been fit for the demands of The Haven — or especially for my association with Lowell. Perhaps, first and foremost, for poor Jeremy's sake even more than my own, I should give up all this striving and struggling and just try to get well.

Hugh would protect and shelter me. No more of this struggle that was wearing me down, only the peace that Hugh was offering . . .

I didn't love him, but surely I could do so in time — when I was apart from Lowell, when I was well again and no longer haunted by the elusive ghost of Robert. It would be so easy to say 'yes' to Hugh and just let everything happen. So very easy to say it now, when I was so tired, when he was so kind . . .

'Are you warm enough?' he was asking. 'Are you comfortable?'

I was comfortable. The upholstery

was deep and soft. I realised, suddenly, how desperately weary I was. When I was well again, no longer floundering in this half-life, then I needn't be a burden to Hugh. He wouldn't need then to hide me and my forlorn confusion away. I might even travel with him, do all I could to help with his work. Was that such an impossible dream?

His arm around me was gentle and sustaining. He had turned on some soft music that surrounded us and eclipsed the awkwardness of silence. I had lost many hours of sleep during so many nights, and now my eyelids were uncontrollably heavy. I tried to say, 'Hugh, I do want to talk to you about everything — but — but — '

I thought he told me just to rest and not worry. I wasn't quite sure what he said or I said. I was drifting, floating, far down into a dark, bottomless well.

How long I slept I never quite knew, but it must have been a considerable while.

Eventually I began dreaming, anxious

fragments of dreams. From one of those I awoke with a great start, aware that the car had stopped moving. I blinked unbelievingly out at The Haven. It seemed an eternity of time since I left it. Children's voices drifted out across the well-kept gardens and tidily-swept paths.

I was suddenly aware of something else as well. The yellow mini-bus was parked in its usual place — which meant Lowell was back. If Hugh intended going inside to see him, the sparks would fly.

'Are you awake?' Hugh said gently. 'I hope you won't mind too much if I rush straight off. I have to be in London tomorrow at the TV studios.'

'Of course,' I muttered. Relief flooded in.

'I hate to leave you, but it won't be for long.' He turned towards me and his hand tilted my face to his. 'I know you've done the right thing, Paula.'

The words puzzled me. But the car door was open and I scrambled out. I saw him wave a farewell hand to Mrs Beecher hovering in the doorway.

Then the car was moving, sliding away down the driveway. There were people fussing round, escorting me inside, clamouring to know where I had been and what it was like to be taken out by a popular idol. In the midst of it all, Sophie gave one of her frantic little screeches.

'Look! Everyone look!' She lapsed into shrill rapid French, and grabbed my hand and held it up for all to see. Like magic a bigger crowd grew, chorusing oohs and aahs of awe and envy.

It was only then that I saw the cause of all this excitement. I saw it, but I was very, very far from understanding.

It was my left hand that Sophie was exhibiting. A beautiful diamond flashed out its incredible message from the third finger.

★ ★ ★

It seemed as though the entire staff of The Haven, and most of the children, too, had me trapped in a great melee of people. If I were dreaming, the dream had become stark nightmare. Voices kept repeating words like 'Wonderful' and 'Fabulous,' calling out 'Congratulations!' and imploring, 'Tell us about it . . .'

How could I explain there was nothing to tell?

Arms squeezed me, eyes peered at that chilly, sparkling stone. I realised all at once I had to be by myself, to cling on to my dwindling sanity. Somehow I had to escape all of them!

It was Mrs Beecher, as excited as anyone, who came to my rescue.

'Poor Paula, all this has been too much for you, and no wonder. Come on, everyone,' she ordered, 'give the girl some peace. We'll hear all the details later on — won't we, Paula?'

I smiled at her, a stiff, forced smile, moving and talking like an automaton. On the pretext of going upstairs to change, I left them behind, still chattering and exclaiming.

As I stumbled upstairs, my head throbbing, it was the final straw when a child blocked my way, insisting on asking me something. I exploded in quite unreasonable anger, 'I can't stop now! Can't you see I can't stop now?'

The flame-haired boy cowered back, his sharp, freckled face suddenly pale and apprehensive. It took quite a lot to alarm Jeremy.

'What's the trouble here?' another authorative voice asked on the landing just above. Whirring along from the lift, Lowell seemed in his usual way to grasp the situation instantly.

'Jeremy, don't worry, I think your mother just isn't feeling so good,' he said reassuringly. 'I'll take care of her. Meantime, why don't you run downstairs for me and tell Mrs Burns I could use some hot coffee?'

'Well. All right.' Jeremy nodded. He didn't sigh or mutter at being given an errand. He seemed quite glad to escape downstairs.

I was still frantic to get to my room, to be alone. But Lowell was barring my way. He said, 'OK, this whole place has turned into a bear-garden — but now we're quiet, so tell me. Tell me what happened to you.'

'I don't know what happened, do you think I'd be in this state if I did?' I flared at him wildly. Then no more words would come, I just stood there, shaking all over with shock.

His hand gripped my arm, not gentle now but hard and unyielding. 'I don't allow hysterics or histrionics from my staff,' he said sharply. 'That's not the sort of example we need to set here. You'd better come with me, Paula.'

'I want to go upstairs! I have to think! I want — '

'I don't care what you want! Just don't give me any arguments.'

I could have hit him, in my frustration. I wanted only to struggle free and escape. But that inexorable grip wouldn't be denied, and I had no strength to resist. He took me the length of the corridor, past bedrooms and bathrooms and a couple of storerooms, round an isolated corner. We reached The Haven's sick-room, at present untenanted.

'Inside!' Lowell directed. As I flopped weakly on one of the beds, he nodded grimly. 'That's better. Now there's just the two of us, no bugs on the walls, no eyes at the window. Now tell me!'

'I'm not surprised your family can't stand living with a bully like you!' I told him.

'We'll leave my home life right out of this.' Momentarily his black eyes glinted. 'Let's talk about you, what kind of shock you had. You did have a shock?'

'Yes, I did!' Suddenly, I thrust my tell-tale hand close to his face. 'I went out in Hugh's car — and when I came back everyone was congratulating me because I had this ring — but I don't remember getting it, I don't remember saying I'd marry him! I — I just don't know any more what's real and what isn't real.'

I was half-crying now. 'Oh, I'll have to leave here, won't I? I'm not responsible for what I do. I — I'm not safe to have around the children.'

'Never mind that. Tell me about Hugh. You remember him asking you to marry him?'

'Oh, he's asked me lots of times. He keeps on asking! And today we were talking in the car, and I thought I could marry him, then he'd leave you and The Haven alone and stop hounding you!' I heard him mutter under his breath something more forceful than elegant. 'But I don't remember saying 'yes' to him! And I must have done that, mustn't I? Oh, I can't go on living like this!' I cried out despairingly.

I hid my face in shaking hands. Dimly I was aware of his chair to-ing and fro-ing, and the chink of a spoon in a glass. I didn't look up. I didn't want to know — until again that strong hand enforced obedience, pulling my fingers away from my face.

'Here's what we'll do, Paula. First of all, get this into your head. If you don't want to marry the guy, you don't have to! You understand that? Now, swallow this down. All of it.'

'I don't want to go to sleep. I have to work things out.'

'Sure you do. But drink this first.'

I drank it. Quite meekly now I accepted his next instruction to lie down here where he could keep an eye on me. 'I can't get up all those damn stairs to the top floor,' he said.

When he left me, I did lie there quite still, staring at my two hands — the left with that flashing diamond, the right with the plain gold band that had been moved there. Robert's ring, summarily displaced. I couldn't remember transferring it. I only knew it seemed a cruel lack of respect to the elusive ghost that was Robert.

Debbie came in soon after with a warm drink and my dressing-gown. She put aside my shoes, hung up my dress, and tucked me up snugly. By now it was becoming an effort to keep my eyes open. I didn't want to sleep, but I slept.

Whatever sedative Lowell had given me brought oblivion for several hours. But eventually, disturbing dreams began to intrude — all of them peopled by a half-heard voice, a faceless shadow of a man who looked at me with Jeremy's grey eyes.

Robert, who I had once loved. Robert, who once had held me in his arms and given me his child. Until I remembered him, could I ever fight off this sickness that was robbing me of my senses? I sat up suddenly in the bed, my eyes wide open.

There was one place where his lost presence had almost become real! One place where I heard his voice in the wash and tumble of the seashore, where the tide and the wind-tossed spray so nearly brought him back. If any place on earth could throw open my shuttered mind, it was that terrifying spot! I had to go there, to find Robert.

An early dawn was lighting the sky, but all was silent in the big house as I pulled on my clothes. Minutes later I was creeping down the stairs in the eerie quiet. Below in the hallway I picked up someone's coat. The fresh chill air of a new morning was filling my lungs. Nothing moved in the shadowy gardens, but leaves in the wind — and the stealthy shape of Cleopatra.

The big gates meant more bolts, but nothing could prevent me now. Out in the empty lane I ran.

All along the sea road with the wind clawing my hair, the gulls calling, the tide thundering below the cliffs, the distance seemed to take for ever. Still running and walking by turns, panting, stumbling, I went on until at last there was a place I recognised, The Maiden's Pool. There was the rough path leading downwards, down to the dark haunted waters of the pool sullenly glimmering below.

'Paula!'

I heard that alien voice, and I heard too an unmistakable whirring. It was impossible, but I heard it. I looked up — and saw Lowell coming towards me from the road. He must have watched me leave the house; he hadn't prevented me but just followed on to see where I went. All this way, while I supposed myself alone, he had somehow trailed along in the rear.

'Go back!' I screamed at him in sudden fierce anger at his intrusion. 'Don't come down here!' The second shout was in urgent fear for him, for the reckless risk he was taking.

He kept on coming. Down the rough path, slithering over the rocks, far too fast. It was inevitable, what happened next. The wheelchair seemed to leap out of his control, rebounding off a boulder, tipping him out violently. He rolled, vainly struggling for a handhold — over the verge of the hollow, down into that supposedly bottomless dark water.

Just one strangled, gurgling cry for

help I heard. The splash of the water, the suddenly ominous call of wheeling gulls, and one human cry.

When I plunged headlong into the water, its bitter chill robbing me momentarily of breath, Lowell's dark head had dipped below the surface. I knew he was a helpless disabled man, and he was drowning. His life was ebbing away before my eyes. And I mustn't let that happen, not to Lowell too, as it had happened to Robert — as I remembered it happening to Robert . . .

I remembered! In those nightmare moments of struggle, of choking blinding salt water and biting cold, clear and vivid there flashed upon my mind the knowledge that this had happened before, this terrible fight with a hungry sea. I saw again the crippled Sea Queen, I heard the last scream of Caroline as the waves tore her from my arms. I saw my last living glimpse of Robert.

'Lowell,' I choked, 'for God's sake

stop struggling, you'll drown us both!'
His frantic grip on me was dragging us
down together — but then mercifully
he became a limp burden in my arms,
and that was just a little easier. But the
edge of this accursed pool and dry land
was still a long, long distance away.

Then I dreamed a dream. I thought I
heard voices, that ready arms and eager
hands were pulling me and my burden
on to the rocks.

⋆   ⋆   ⋆

When I'd arrived on my dazed flight
from The Haven, I hadn't noticed a
caravan parked for an overnight stop.
But there it was, and here were its
occupants — a man and a woman and
two sons, all in varied states of
dishabille and excitement, who had
been roused by a peculiar whirring of
wheels close to their resting place. Now
they had completely taken over the
situation.

I found myself being smothered in

coats and blankets, showered with sympathy and praise for what they kept calling great bravery.

'Never mind me, I'm all right. Just help him, please look after him first,' I told them.

Then another voice said, 'Hi, Paula.' A voice I had never really expected to hear again.

He should be inert on the ground, with frantic rescuers fighting to pump breath into his body. Yet he was sitting in his chair, drenched, shivering, but open-eyed and coherent. The family of campers, even more horrified to find he had actually fallen from an up-ended wheelchair, had righted that long-suffering chariot and lifted him aboard.

Now we were alone, the family having gone into the caravan to prepare hot soup for us.

I could only give thanks for his amazing powers of recuperation. I had other things on my mind now — and Lowell had even recovered enough to sense this in his uncanny way. I was shaking with cold, with shock, and with all the anger of my awakened memory.

'Tell me, Paula,' he said softly.

'I'll tell you! I've remembered — it was Robert who saved Jeremy, and I went after Caroline but — but I couldn't hold on to her. Robert came to help me, then he was swept away too . . .'

'Where was Hugh?'

'He saved himself. Just himself!' I almost spat out the words. 'That's all he did!'

I knew now why Hugh had wanted to hide me away from an inquisitive world, the world he had allowed to think him a hero and credit him with an act of selfless bravery. That supposed heroism had helped to build up his public image, just as his attentive care of me, bereaved and sick, had helped it still more.

But he dared not let me remember! It was really so simple, so very obvious. He would go to any lengths — even marriage — to get me safely hidden away, especially away from Lowell's attempts to restore my memory in case I ever recalled that Hugh Egerton was a coward who thought only of preserving his own idolised skin, a coward who had lived and was still living a gross lie . . .

My anger turned to the sheer misery of this cold, drenched moment of bitter revelation.

'How could he?'

In my sick disillusion, only the strong grip of Lowell's hand on mine sustained me.

7

'Now mind you finish all that soup, dear,' Mrs Bissett ordered me. 'Shall I find you another blanket? Lowell, are you sure you're warm enough?'

We both assured her meekly that we were warm. She was very kind, but exhausting. That description in fact applied to the whole Bissett tribe. Marion and George were fortyish, lean and fit, and well into jogging, marathon — running, and rock-climbing as well as spartan caravanning holidays with chilly muesli breakfasts. Their two early-teenage boys, Brian and Malcolm, were growing up like young oak trees.

Marion had loaned me a cerise track-suit. I was past caring about the horrific clash of the vivid pink with my flame-coloured hair. I was dry, combed and clad, provided amply with scalding soup and wholemeal bread.

I couldn't see much of Lowell, who was sitting on a bunk opposite, except a mummy-like swathing of plaid blankets, from out of which his black curly hair damply surmounted the strong, dark face touched with a similar wry glimmer of humour. The Bissetts evidently amused him, too.

He had come up with a glib explanation for their benefit, that I had lost something on the shore and come to look for it, and he had rashly followed on to help. Doubtless they supposed it was a watch or some jewellery I was seeking. No one would have thought I was searching for a memory.

'Anyway,' Lowell assured them, 'she found it — so I guess the dawn swim was worthwhile!'

Marion, still much concerned, was thinking of calling a doctor.

Lowell countered that effectively. 'You're speaking to a doctor,' he told her. 'And my friend here is a nurse.

We're a mine of medical know-how between us.'

Mrs Bissett's expression rather indicated that in that case we should both have had more sense.

After a few minutes the two of us were left briefly alone in the caravan while the Bissetts bustled around outside. They were examining Lowell's wheelchair, which seemed finally to have given up the ghost, and clearing the big estate car ready to transport it and us home. Between whiles, Lowell surmised, they were probably climbing the cliffs blindfolded by way of a little gentle exercise.

I laughed — and I shouldn't have done, because the laugh broke into a sob.

The front I had somehow presented to the strangers collapsed abruptly.

'I know,' Lowell said, exactly as though I had spoken my thoughts aloud. 'It's like waking from a long sleep.'

It was a sad awakening. Tears welled

in my eyes as I recalled that other tragic struggle in a wild, hungry sea which had ended my last holiday with Robert. Maybe Hugh could have helped me save him, maybe prevented, too, the loss of poor Caroline who could have been his bride. He might have done, if he had tried.

'He wouldn't help,' I whispered. 'I kept screaming at him — but he just saved himself and watched me trying to help them. Yes, he watched when they died, he watched them both die! And that's the great public hero who's always extolling Christian principles, the man everyone admires so much they dip into their pockets for all his charity appeals — '

This time I didn't feel the rending bitterness of my first remembrance. That fierce anger against Hugh Egerton, so great a hypocrite, had faded now into all-encompassing grief.

'I thought so. I thought it happened that way,' Lowell said quietly.

'You did? You really guessed?'

'There had to be some reason why he wanted to bury you away. He couldn't risk you remembering, could he? And after going through the motions with all the conventional guys who very conveniently failed to cure your amnesia, he couldn't chance some way-out Moroni treatment doing it for them. It all figures.'

It did figure. I could only wonder that my own blindness had lasted so long. I could only marvel, too, that I had ever forgotten the man I loved and married and lost.

'Tell me about him,' Lowell said, again uncannily reading my thoughts.

He knew I desperately needed to talk now, to bring into the open the vivid. memory of my life with Robert — the love we had shared in those busy, laughing, labouring student days against the background of the teeming hospital and our own little home. The warm, cluttered little flat that had been our refuge, where the lights kept fusing, and you could hardly turn round in the kitchen where I made quick fry-ups and Robert always bumped his head on an awkward water-pipe.

How we'd held each other joyously, protectively close during the nights when we were both off duty . . .

But there had been storms as well as love. My quick temper had flared when Robert misunderstood and aggravated me, and his chilly maddening sulks deepened when I'd misunderstood and aggravated him. We'd fought at first half in fun, and as time went by too often in earnest.

Even the wonder of Jeremy's birth and first precious years hadn't healed for long the canker at the root of our joint lives when we'd snatched the time for the brief Cornish holiday together. It was a desperate attempt to save a tottering marriage.

An attempt that still hadn't succeeded on the day of the doomed Sea Queen trip. Robert, who disliked boats and boating, hadn't wanted to go and my temper had flared. I'd accused him of being a sulky spoil-sport who ruined everything I tried to do. His grey eyes had been hard and angry — the look I had seen lately in Jeremy's eyes.

So we'd gone on our boat trip. In front of Hugh, Caroline, and Jeremy we'd pretended to enjoy the outing, privately furious with each other, exchanging belligerent glances and mutterings. The last quarrel, the very last.

'All my fault,' I declared shakily now — all mine, as so many others were!

I wept now in deep sorrow as I remembered across the years all the guilt and the grief that came to me when Robert was torn away from me in the cruel sea. Our final parting in the midst of conflict, with no time for any farewell, no forgiving reunion.

I recalled those last brief moments before the mocking waves tossed me headlong against a rock so that pain made my mind blank. If Hugh had managed then to hoist the bleeding and bereaved ghost of me to safety beside him — with no great risk to deter him — he'd scarcely done me a favour. It was too late to tell Robert that I loved him. Too late ever to beg Robert to forgive me as I'd forgiven him and let us start again . . .

'Too late,' Lowell echoed the words softly beside me. 'They're the saddest words ever spoken. Paula, I was so afraid of this, I was so sure your problems came from more than Robert's death alone. I'm an expert on the ways a marriage can crumble, unfortunately. I've been there. So now you can understand it was the remorse as well as the sorrow that forced your mind to black out, because it was simply too painful to remember. It's quite a classic syndrome. But that makes it no easier.'

I couldn't look at him. I could only sob in naked helplessness. It was then that somehow arms reached out to me, and received me, and held me fast. I clung to him, and great rending sobs drained some of the unbearable pain from me. Just dimly, I felt a lingering hand caressing my hair. I felt the touch of his face against mine.

In these past weeks I had dreamed, guiltily, of holding Lowell close to my empty heart. Now, on this day when the two of us had looked upon sudden death, when miraculously light had penetrated my shattered mind, the impossible had come true. In our weird garb and swathing blankets, I was locked in his arms and he rocked me and soothed me so gently, so very gently. And it was only of Robert I thought, only for Robert I ached and wept.

'If I could just've told him I really loved him — if I could only be sure he knew that,' I said softly.

'He knew. Believe me. He knew.'

I wanted to believe.

I gave a long shuddering sigh and lifted my head. If Robert had known, that was something to hold on to. That was the greatest comfort I could find.

* * *

'Well, everything is certainly happening today, folks!' Marion bustled in, making me hastily avert my tear-wet face. 'Quite a lot of smoke going up from somewhere quite near, it must be a fair-sized fire!'

'Just along the coast,' her husband confirmed. 'Could be a big hotel, I suppose.'

'Dad,' Malcolm clamoured, 'can we go and see the fire?'

The Bissetts, their morning already well disrupted, were in a welter of new excitement. I looked at Lowell and saw his face suddenly pale.

'Which direction along the coast?' he asked tersely.

'That way!' Brian waved a hand.

I met Lowell's eyes. In that instant, torn abruptly from my own personal tragedy, the same apprehension clawed into me. He was already throwing off his blanket cocoon.

'Let's get the car started — right now!' he rapped at a startled Mr Bissett. 'And can someone give me a hand down from this damn trailer? Come on, let's go! It could be The Haven clinic, we've a dozen handicapped patients there.'

Afterwards, I was never sure quite how Lowell got down from the caravan and into the roomy estate car. Somehow, we were all packed into the car and it bumped and jolted over the uneven ground and on to the road.

It was still early morning, clear and bright now, a beautiful new day. Gulls wheeled and called over the cliffs, the unsleeping tide thundered below. All along this road I had panted and laboured an hour or two ago. Now, squeezed between Lowell and Brian, I watched the picturesque vistas fly past the car windows.

The children, my terrified thoughts kept repeating — the children, who couldn't cope with life, who couldn't run to safety! My own son, Jeremy, Robert's son, whose short life had already overflowed with tragedy . . .

'It has to be The Haven.' I heard

Lowell's terse comment as we came nearer to the ominous smoke. 'I hope to God they've remembered the fire drill.'

A turn or two of the road and I saw the familiar gates, the painted name-board — and the spreading bulk of the building shrouded in smoke. Milling children were trembling with shock or sobbing in terror, some clutching treasured possessions, some clinging to members of staff scarcely less distressed.

I was looking for Jeremy's red-gold head and I couldn't see it. Before the car stopped I scrambled out and ran.

I shouted his name over and over. 'Jeremy! Where's Jeremy? Has anyone seen . . . ?'

I realised now that the fire seemed to be centred on the tower wing, normally locked up and disused. I saw, too, unbelievably, a large, sleek, black car parked on the lawn. Hugh's car!

'Oh, Paula, you're here.' Faye Prescott, her hair for once a ruin around her ashen face, grabbed my arm. It was

Faye, I saw dimly, who was performing the Herculean job of marshalling everyone into orderly groups on the grass at a safe distance. 'We found Lowell's note that you'd both gone out — is he back, too?'

'He's in the car.' I waved an impatient hand. 'Where's Jeremy? I can't find — '

'Annie,' Faye called to Mrs Beecher, 'come and talk to Paula here!' She was already fleeing across to the Bissetts' car.

'Oh, my dear!' Annie Beecher, a bulky figure in a candlewick dressing-gown, her plump, kindly face begrimed, had three children safely in tow, Bridget, Ben, and Camilla. 'Such a terrible thing! Two of the children must have started the fire somehow in the tower and they're still up there now. And, Paula, your fiancé just drove in a moment ago and he rushed straight up there to try to reach them.'

'He's ace!' Camilla breathed in tremulous rapture. 'Just like Superman.'

'The others were trying to get to them, but it's the smoke and those narrow stairs,' Annie continued. 'Don't you worry, though, the Fire Brigade will be here any minute and they'll soon get the poor little mites out safely!'

She sounded as though she was trying to convince herself.

'Jeremy?' I asked, but I knew already.

'I'm sorry, dear. Yes, Jeremy and Tony. But the firemen will get them out, Paula.'

I heard Faye's voice again, as she came running back. 'Look, Hugh's at the top, he's with the boys. So no more panic, everyone, just stay back and keep still!'

In flat contravention of those so sensible orders, I pushed and shoved rapidly through the watching throng, right over to the stricken smoke-shrouded tower wing. And now I saw the motley band of helpers who were labouring there.

Mrs Burns and Morgan between them held steady a ladder to the roof of an extension building. The grim house-keeper, her head bristling with old-fashioned metal curlers, was gazing up in a mixture of fear and pride at her husband, who was there on the roof with slender, agile Sophie, for once minus her three-inch heels. They had dragged a mattress up on to the flat roof.

Joe Burns, that worried little man, amazingly cool and collected in this life-and-death struggle, was shouting huskily upwards to the height of the burning tower. 'We're ready! We're ready for you!'

'We 'ave ze bed ready!' Sophie screamed in chorus.

Mrs Burns grabbed me with an iron hand, preventing me rushing up the ladder, too. 'No, Paula, you'll get in Joe's way. Leave it to my Joe.'

I glimpsed, at a small top window where smoke billowed, Hugh leaning far out. He held a frantic, struggling Tony. Then, the boy plummetted down, his fall safely broken by Joe and Sophie and the mattress. Behind me, there was the clamour of a fire engine, nearer and nearer. I didn't even turn towards the gates as it bowled through.

I saw Hugh, choking, scarlet-faced, was holding another child, a bright-haired child.

With Morgan's bulk weighting the ladder, his full-moon face a mask of horror and effort, my hands and Mrs Burns' received from Sophie the now half-insensible Tony. Jeremy had landed successfully on the roof. The boys were dirty, terrified and gasping for air, but they were safe.

Joe shouted urgently upwards, 'Come on, sir! Jump!'

'Hugh.' I choked.

I saw him a moment more, there at the high window. There was the fierce crackle of old wood burning like tinder, and stifling smoke. Voices behind me were shouting orders.

Hugh had climbed into the window opening when I heard him cry out, a cry of sheer terror. Through the fog of smoke, I saw the sudden flare-up as something caved in, turning the top of the battlemented tower into flames.

There was no Hugh at the window now. There was no window.

'My God,' Mrs Burns muttered beside me. 'Oh, my God.'

★   ★   ★

I cradled Jeremy in my arms. For one brief moment, I closed my eyes on the drama all around, now completely in the charge of the professional firefighters, and gave thanks for the life of my son.

He looked so very small, still trembling and gasping. His face was Robert's face, those grey eyes, those features so clearly in the mould of his father's. How could I have looked at our son and not seen and remembered Robert?

There were two ambulances now ready and waiting, but mercifully they weren't receiving too many casualties.

The fire had centred on that one section of the building, the children had been hastily evacuated, so the human damage was confined mostly to shock, the effects of smoke, and minor bumps sustained in the rush to safety. Two or three were being taken to the Penvor Hospital for attention — including, of course, Jeremy and Tony, whose conditions were more serious.

But now another victim was being hurried to an ambulance. I surrendered Jeremy to other ready, helping hands and started shakily forward towards the still figure under the blankets. With deepest pain and horror, I saw Hugh's fair, handsome face blackened and disfigured, the honey-blond hair raggedly scorched.

'Hugh,' I whispered.

The attendants had paused to load him into the ambulance, and I bent over him, ignoring whatever they said to me. Far, far away now was that wild and bitter anger of an hour go. 'Hugh, it's Paula, can you hear me? Hugh, thank you — thank you for Jeremy . . . '

I touched his forehead very softly with my lips. The closed eyes just flickered. There was a light of recognition, quickly lost again.

'Please stand away!' someone ordered me.

There was no help I could give Hugh just now except to pray for him, hope for him. From the bottom of a heart overflowing, I hoped and prayed.

Nor, indeed, could I do much yet for Jeremy, who was in good hands and had the company of other children and Mrs Beecher. A little later I would go to the hospital. Meantime, there was so much to do here, so much help I could give to others.

As though with life reborn, I was filled with a strange surge of energy and eagerness. Quickly I was immersed, unwearied and clear-headed, in the urgent necessities all around me. In this strange transformation from my confusion of months and years, I even found myself issuing orders, taking charge along with Faye and Lowell.

Faye glanced at me once or twice in amazement.

Lowell, now mobile again in his spare hand-propelled wheelchair which had been retrieved from somewhere showed no surprise.

By this time, sightseers had congregated, not to mention a contingent from the local newspaper. I hurried here and there, rescuing belongings, despatching the remaining children and escorting staff to hotels in St Owen to await collection by their families. Several bystanders, as well as the ever-helpful Bissetts, provided lifts.

The fire was already out, leaving a maze of hoses and still eddying smoke. Gradually, with the children safely departed, the scene was resolving into order. I couldn't bear to look at The Haven, the object of such high hopes and such long and dedicated work.

The building that now should be abuzz with morning life, stood there gaunt and void, part of it blackened and gutted. Scarcely too could I bear to look at Lowell, who was everywhere, his face by now grey and aged with exhaustion.

For once, he looked a defeated man. The force that drove him to surmount all obstacles and fight all foes, seemed to have drained away in the drifting smoke.

'My fault, of course,' I heard him saying to Faye. 'I wasn't giving a hundred per cent concentration last night — so I didn't check properly that the tower was locked up after it was used yesterday. So we've gone up in smoke. And it could have cost lives, it very nearly cost three — '

'Lowell, don't talk like that. You mustn't blame yourself,' Faye protested.

'Of course not, no one could have foreseen that those boys would set the tower alight,' I chimed in. 'What were they doing, smoking cigarettes on the quiet?'

'I don't know what they were doing,'

Lowell said shortly. 'I do know I'm in charge of the place so the responsibility was mine. Or I was in charge,' he added with bitterness, as he glanced at the stricken building. So, obviously he believed this blow to the already threatened Haven must be its final death-thrust.

I could find nothing to say that wouldn't be a banal platitude. How could you say 'Never mind' to someone whose life-work had collapsed around their ears? In any case, he didn't wait for any kind of solace, hastily wheeling his chair away from us.

Faye glanced at me. She said shakily, 'This is going to kill him by inches. It's started already.'

'I know. Because this isn't just a job for him, is it? It's his purpose in living, he gave up his music for it, he gave up his family . . . ' If I were betraying confidences I didn't even realise it. I was near to tears.

'Paula, don't wait around any longer, you've done more than your share. I know you want to get along to the hospital.' Faye squeezed my arm. 'We can manage here.'

'Well, if you're sure.'

She was sure. Whatever my past opinion of her, today I knew she would help Lowell until she dropped. The Bissetts' car had just returned after ferrying some of the children to the village, and George Bissett said they would drop me at Penvor Hospital.

Someone had told them it was actually Hugh Egerton who was badly hurt. Did I happen to know?

I confirmed briefly that Hugh had visited The Haven clinic several times. They tut-tutted about the man who did such marvellous work being injured in the line of duty.

I parried all their other questions, just longing now to reach the town. So far I hadn't allowed myself to think about Hugh, or to dwell on my last glimpse of him. This familiar road made me think of the regular Haven shopping trips in the mini-bus, and my first worried visit here with poor Bridget — and later the nightmare search for three runaways. All of it seemed an eternity ago.

When we reached the green-painted railings fronting the hospital, I assured the Bissetts they mustn't wait. I had their address so I could send a replacement of the pink tracksuit. Privately, I resolved to send a gift for the boys, too. The family had been a godsend to me today.

I was soon swallowed up into the busy world of the hospital, sitting on a chilly, plastic chair, watching the other people waiting, and the brisk, blue-and-white nurses. Instantly, there flooded through my mind a host of clear and vivid memories, the years when I wore one of those uniforms, when I was part of a world like this. Oh, so many memories.

I remembered kissing Robert good-bye when I rushed off for my duty shift, and falling into bed beside him when I came home late and exhausted. Also the day when there was an unusual visitor to the children's ward, a raven-haired man in a wheelchair, who was so absorbed in the little Indian girl called Rashida. He asked me countless questions and insisted on answers.

He got in my way all morning and didn't apologise. He held Rashida's little hand so very gently in his, and smiled into the crippled child's huge, frightened eyes, until he actually coaxed from her a smile in return.

'Mrs Hastings,' a voice called me. 'Will you come this way?'

* * *

'Here's your mummy, Jeremy, so cheer up now,' the fresh-faced nurse said. She had freckles, and strands of red hair sprouted rebelliously from under her sedate little white hat. 'Mrs Hastings, he's going to be just fine — only quite minor burns and bruises. Dr Deacon says you can take him home tomorrow, or maybe even later today with a bit of luck.'

'Good, that's wonderful,' I said inadequately. 'And do you know about the other little boy, Tony Abbot?'

She did know. Tony was up in a ward, suffering chiefly from the effects of smoke and a fractured wrist sustained in his drop to safety. He was quite comfortable.

She left me alone with Jeremy, bustling off to see if Dr Deacon could have a talk with me. We were in a small treatment room, and Jeremy lay beneath a blanket, a bandaged arm stuck out stiffly beside him. There was no doubt he had come through this horrific experience well. Jeremy was a born survivor. He had needed to be.

He looked at me now, so clearly anticipating all sorts of angry recriminations. Instead, I tugged a chair close to him and quietly reached for the small uninjured hand. It instinctively clenched away from me.

'It's all right. Jeremy, it's all right,' I

told him quietly. 'I'm just very, very glad you're not hurt badly. And, listen to me, I have something to tell you. You know I've been sick, don't you? I'm sure you couldn't understand why I'd turned into a different person all this while. Well, I'm better, darling. I'm really better. I'm Mum again. Oh, I know things can never be the same as when we had poor Daddy with us, but we have each other, and we have Auntie Penny . . . '

Quite suddenly, the hardness in his eyes began melting into tears. For all the dramas and traumas of his short life, he was really a hurt, bewildered little boy.

My own voice almost broke as I went on. 'You had such a bad time, and I wasn't able to help you. But, in future, things will be different. They really will!'

He nodded, as though half-believing. Other things were on his mind. He burst out, 'Me and Tony, we never meant to start the fire.'

'I'm sure you didn't mean to. Would you like to tell me about it?'

He told me in a sudden half-coherent rush of words. It was Tony's idea, but he had needed no persuading, he admitted freely — and they had bribed Morgan with some sweets Tony received from home, only Morgan had backed out at the last minute. All they intended was to try out Tony's idea of making the tower into a beacon light.

Mrs Burns kept an emergency store of candles, and Joe had a couple of lanterns for similar contingencies in his tool-shed. The conspirators managed to 'nick them,' as Jeremy put it, last evening, along with matches from pipe-smoker Joe's jacket which he conveniently left hanging somewhere. When they found the tower door left unlocked, it seemed the heavens were smiling on them.

The rest hardly needed telling. Rather later than the boys planned, as early daylight dawned, they began setting up their beacon. Morgan, who refused to venture up the rather spooky shadowy tower, finally agreed to go outside to see how the signal looked.

So it was Morgan who gave the alarm when things got out of hand. The hazardous operation had ignited first an old carton on which the candles were placed, then the dry old timbers and a store of decorating materials kept there. The boys had attempted to beat out the fire, but only succeeded in spreading it.

They'd tried to flee to safety, but the narrow stairs were speedily engulfed in smoke — and Tony, of course, with his twisted legs that had first led to his presence at The Haven, couldn't run anyway. It was a wonder that Jeremy had ever managed to help him up the stairs in the first place.

Once fairly started, the fire spread incredibly fast. If Morgan hadn't roused the household, the consequences would have been far worse.

'We didn't mean to,' Jeremy kept repeating. 'And now the house is all burned, and it was all our fault. Do you think Dr Moroni will tell the police it was us and they'll come and take us away?'

I held him in my arms. It was all I could do not to crush him against me with all the pent-up love and longing of this strange reunion.

I didn't want to frighten him with my newly-awakened emotions. He had been through enough today. There would be plenty of time now for the two of us.

'Dr Moroni is very upset,' I told him gently. 'You must tell him later all you've told me and how sorry you are. He'll understand, Jeremy, I know he will.'

I told him, too, that of course he and Tony did wrong to trespass in a forbidden area and help themselves from forbidden stores. But they couldn't have foreseen the consequences. They had learned a hard lesson.

Jeremy sighed shakily. 'I hated that Haven. I always hoped it would get blown up, but now I — I'm sort of sorry it's all spoiled. Where will everyone go?' he fretted. 'And, oh, what happened to Cleopatra, and the fish, and Tubby and Cuddles?'

I was telling him the cat, fish, and rabbits had been saved when we were interrupted by Dr Deacon, who turned out to be a business-like young lady.

Jeremy seemed to have had a lucky escape, she confirmed, and I could take him home shortly. Home.

I thought with a sudden sharp pang, where was home now? We obviously couldn't go to The Haven, so that meant Penny in London, at least for the present. Already today my world had turned on its axis. I couldn't think yet beyond the here and now.

Before I quite steeled my courage to ask about Hugh, the doctor forestalled me. He was incessantly asking for 'Paula,' she said.

'Oh, that's me!' I exclaimed foolishly.

'Well, they want you upstairs, Mrs Hastings. The new wing, I'll show you.

We don't often get famous personalities here,' she added. 'Do you know, there's a hoard of newsmen and cameras being held at bay down there in reception?'

'It's always like that with Hugh,' I said. 'Is he going to be all right?'

She declined to give any details, just directing me where to go. I told Jeremy I wouldn't be long, and followed the directions, chilled through suddenly with a cold weight of dread. This was the end of thrusting the thought of Hugh far back in my mind.

When another nurse took me to a private room opening off a cream-painted corridor, I was suddenly near to breaking down. Perhaps it wasn't surprising, after all that the last frantic 24 hours had held for me. I was being told that Mr Egerton's condition was serious but stable. It was essential that he rested and my visit must be brief. I could see him for just a few minutes.

Inside the room where Hugh lay, I needed no one to tell me he was very ill. I noticed the equipment around his bed, the paraphernalia once so familiar to me. I saw the face that was so changed and the eyes dulled by pain and drugs. Yet there was consciousness and recognition in them, looking straight up into mine.

'Here you are, Mrs Hastings,' the nurse said.

I sat on the chair she had pulled near.

'Paula, I had to see you,' he said quite clearly. 'I — I have things to say . . . '

'Later, when you're better.' I tried to hush him. 'Hugh, I'm so very, very sorry you were hurt — and I just don't know how to say thank you for the way you saved the boys, there aren't any words. I've just seen Jeremy, he's fine and I'll bring him to see you as soon as he's allowed. Now, I mustn't stay, just tell me if there's anything I can do or anyone I can call. Your aunt, or do you want to see anyone from the studios?'

He wasn't listening, rejecting all that restively. 'Come nearer,' he whispered urgently. 'I have to say this and you're too far away . . . '

I bent closer to please him, because his voice was very weak. I had to let him speak. To refuse would only add to his distress.

Only part of the muttered, jumbled words I clearly understood, but they were enough. The confused story he tried to tell me added more light to this day of revelation.

Yesterday, after our drive together, he had been returning to London, but it seemed that at some stage he'd reached a kind of breaking point. Overnight, he drove back towards Cornwall — because finally he had to confess to me how greatly he had deceived me. Over many weeks he had schemed and plotted to persuade me into marriage. All, he admitted, in order to keep safe his guilty secret about the boat disaster. The rescue attempt that day had been accomplished by myself and by Robert — Hugh had completely panicked and thought no further than his own safety. It was just as I had already remembered this morning when light broke through to me in the struggle to save Lowell in the Maiden's Pool.

It was just as Lowell, with his uncanny perception of human frailties, had previously guessed.

'Hugh, please, don't say any more,' I told him. But he wouldn't be stopped. His voice went on. Later, when he was acclaimed a hero by the world for saving my life and Jeremy's, he was tortured by shame and regret, but couldn't face admitting the truth.

His great fear was that I would regain my memory of his cowardice — so the simplest way out was to make me his wife, then I would be completely under his protection and guidance and he could keep me carefully isolated. He even admitted lulling me to sleep and slipping an engagement ring on my finger. No wonder I had thought myself crazy, no wonder I couldn't account for that ring. He deliberately confused my mind in other ways, so that eventually I would be glad just to retreat to the safe, beautiful home he planned for me.

But last night he'd reached the point where he could no longer bear to sail under those false colours. If confession ruined his reputation, his career, his whole life, that was no more than the ruin he had brought to others, he tried to tell me now. And today his decision was still as strong; he knew there would be reporters about and he told me to send them in so he could tell them the truth. That was all he wanted now, to end every deception and stop living this great soul-destroying lie.

I had to let him stumble through to the bitter end. But then, I knew what to say.

'Hugh, I'm glad you told me. Especially because I've started remembering things for myself. And I can understand you had to tell someone, you couldn't keep it to yourself for ever — but listen to me, no one outside this room need ever know. What good will it do us to resurrect the past? Will it bring back Robert for me, or Caroline for you? You mustn't wreck all the work you do, it's far too important.'

He tried to stop me, but it was my turn to speak without interruption. 'Besides,' I hurried on, 'whatever happened in the past, today you were truly a hero, you risked your life to save the boys. I owe Jeremy's life to you, Hugh. What more could you do for me than that?'

I had laid my hand on his arm. I wasn't prepared for him to lift his head with momentary strength and touch my hand with his lips. It was only then that I realised the bright glitter of the diamond was missing. His ring must have left my finger somewhere in the cold haunted depths of the Maiden's Pool.

'We aren't really engaged, then — are we?' I asked nervously.

'No, we're not engaged. But I love you, Paula. Can you believe that? Oh, I didn't when I first planned to marry you, but now I do . . . '

Already his brief strength was fading and his head sank back. I bent closer to hear the other words he said. 'Paula, darling, can you ever forgive me? Can you — think of starting over again?'

If I had answered, he wouldn't have heard. I kissed him.

The nurse was hovering around, telling me I had already overstayed my visit.

Suddenly, I was utterly weary. I could hardly put one foot before the other, to get out of the room and into the corridor.

Please God, Hugh would recover fully and in due time would become absorbed again in his own busy world. Could I really forgive him enough to become his wife and take my place for always at his side? Could I live my life with him, aid him in his work, try to love him as I believed he now loved me?

Was that, after all, the way my tangled future would finally work itself out?

★   ★   ★

That very same day I went back to London. Of all things wonderful, my sister Penny had arrived to collect me.

It seemed that last night, after Lowell calmed my hysteria, he rang her to say I was unwell and it might help if she came down. She arrived to find with horror the sad state of The Haven. She was sent on to the hospital with instructions to ferry me straight back home in a hired car already booked.

'But . . . ' I hesitated, my joy at seeing Penny dimmed by stark realisation that my job at The Haven was over. 'How can I walk out on Lowell when there's so much to do?'

'He told me that if you object I'm to knock you over the head and shanghai you. Or else he'll do it for me!' Penny said sternly.

'And he would, too!' I exploded. 'He's impossible to reason with, I've told him so several times!' I added with almost desperate concern, 'Penny, did you see him? Is he all right? How did he look?'

She had seen him only briefly. He had plenty of help, she assured me, especially a Miss Prescott who was handling official inquiries, Press statements, and anxious parents with equal ease. I was glad he had Faye. This was no moment for futile jealousies.

Faye would be far more use than I could be now. In my present mental and physical exhaustion, even while I protested that I couldn't leave, I longed to seize this chance to escape.

In another hour I had been hustled out by a rear door to sink into the upholstery of a waiting car, with a very subdued Jeremy nestled against me and Penny hanging on to any parts of me she could. She kept gazing into my face, her bright, blue eyes alight with the excitement of finding her sister whole again. Her joy, of course, was tempered with distress about her idolised Hugh.

'I know you're worried about leaving him, Paula,' she kept repeating, 'but he'd want you to go home and rest

— and I'm sure he'll be all right. He just has to be!'

I was pleased when Jeremy fell asleep and it wasn't long before an aching weight of weariness closed my own eyes, too. Thereafter, I knew little about that long, confused drive. I slept on and off most of the time, only wakening to see daylight become hurrying darkness and dazzling head-lamps.

In a dream I heard Penny say, 'We're home, love.' Someone helped me into the dark, empty street. There were rows of tall houses and this one had a welcoming light in the hall.

'Hello, Kevin,' I mumbled, recognising Penny's tall, bearded boyfriend, for once minus his crash helmet.

I let him take me inside and ply me with some sort of hot drink. Jeremy had already been spirited away. Then there was a bedroom, and Robert's desk, Robert's library of books . . .

'Now don't worry about a thing, you hear me?' Penny fussed round me although my dear, caring little sister knew only half of what I'd been through during these past hours and days. 'Your own bed, Paula, all ready for you!'

My own bed, my own things, my own memories. I had come back to them all. Warmth and comfort flooded through me at last. I slept again.

When consciousness ebbed back, broad daylight shone in the familiar room. No Haven attic, no children's voices, no cries of wild, wheeling gulls. Through a gap in the curtains, I glimpsed London pavements and passing traffic.

'Oh, you're awake!' Penny came hurrying in with a pile of newspapers and a breakfast tray. 'How do you feel? Jeremy is lots better, Linda took him upstairs with Adam — we thought it would take his mind off things. Oh, and we spoke to the hospital, and Hugh had quite a peaceful night they said.'

It was quite late afternoon. Yesterday was a far-off dream. But still, as I looked around me, I knew the long-erased past was clear in my mind. I sat up limply, propped on pillows, and to please Penny, I tried to eat. I glanced at the newspapers, all with pictures of Hugh and glowing variations of what had happened at the clinic. I wasn't sure I wanted to read them.

'That suitcase.' I pointed across the room, still absorbed in my flooding recollections. 'Robert kept it under the bed, full of books. I used to moan about it.'

'You really remember everything again?' Penny marvelled. 'The old house, and Mum and Dad? Oh, I rang him, and he's coming down to see you. Very soon.'

I nodded absently, gazing now at the photographs around the room. I was still leafing wistfully through an old album Penny handed me, when there was a disturbance outside. I heard doors opening and voices.

Kevin called out, 'Paula?' and tapped on the bedroom door.

Penny whipped it open sharply. 'Kevin, if that's more reporters, tell them to get lost! Paula is feeling limp.'

'No, it's some people from The Haven,' Kevin explained mildly. 'There's Dr Thingamy — out there in a car, and someone else. But if Paula isn't well enough . . . '

In an instant, with all weariness gone, I had clutched a blanket around me and made a dive for the window. Scarcely conscious of my heart leaping like a wild thing, I pulled back the curtain. The 'someone else' was Faye, very much her elegant self again. I saw her silver-grey Ford squeezed into the inevitable line of parked vehicles, so she must have driven Lowell here.

As I watched, she was helping her passenger with difficulty on to the pavement. I saw him hand out a paper-sheathed spray of flowers, which Faye tucked under her arm for safe-keeping. She looked very serious, very subdued.

But it wasn't Faye Prescott I really

saw. Today I was fully myself, my mind had thrown off its fogs of confusion and was crystal-clear, and I looked out now at Lowell with a love and longing that filled my whole being.

I knew this was the man I loved and would love always! This man who had often made me so utterly angry and yet just as often had helped me with a human understanding deeper than words . . . Lowell, with all his arrogance and intolerance, and his splendid ideas for unfortunate children and the music in his soul he had chosen to deny. The smiles he gave that masked his own bitter secret of loneliness . . .

'They're just stopping by, they can't stay long,' Kevin was telling me. 'He's on his way to catch a plane, you see.'

'A plane?' I asked, wondering.

'I think he's going to Italy,' the amiable, unknowing Kevin rambled on. 'I think they said he's joining his wife who lives there. Does that make sense to you?'

'Yes. Yes, that makes sense,' I heard

304

my own voice say across a void.

'Well, don't stand there rabbiting on, Kevin, give the man a hand up the steps while I put the kettle on,' Penny said. 'Paula, love, does your boss drink tea?'

'Coffee,' that same robot voice said. 'Too much coffee. Too strong.'

I was going to say, 'And he isn't my boss any more. He isn't my anything.' But she had already fled, propelling Kevin before her.

Alone in the room, I went on standing there. I let the curtain drop back. My hands, gripping the window ledge, were ice-cold.

My love for Robert was past, my love for Hugh had never been. My love for Lowell was real and strong and near. It would have been better not to see him again.

Yesterday The Haven had died — and today, secretly and silently, I would die a death of my own.

8

Faye Prescott tapped on the bedroom door as I hastily finished dressing.

'Do come in, but please excuse everything! I'm a bit of a wreck today,' I apologised.

'Aren't we all, my dear?' Faye said. She didn't look a wreck to me, just very much her elegant ash-blonde self. Yet there was a change in her, I thought. Her expression was serious, her manner subdued.

I was bursting with questions to ask her, but something held me back.

'Well, this isn't easy to say, so I wanted to see you alone,' she began abruptly. 'Paula, I'm sorry for — oh, for quite a lot of things. Hugh kept on insisting everything we did was for your good in the long run. Maybe he was right, but — '

'You — and Hugh? I don't understand.' I said. Yet, I was beginning to understand, even before her somewhat tangled explanations.

She had been Hugh's collaborator, his on-the-spot contact at The Haven. It was Faye who had assisted him with his campaign against the clinic. It was Faye who had leaked the news to The Examiner about children being lost late at night, and other details. Faye, too, had helped to make me feel my state of mind was far worse than it really was. She had arranged a string of skilful, false messages, including the one concerning Penny's mythical weekend visit to Cornwall — which a couple of days ago had me doubting my own sanity and ready to do anything Hugh wanted me to do.

'In case you're wondering how I got so involved with him,' she added, 'we've chatted a great many times lately — when he rang and I answered the phone. Later, he gave me a number where I could reach him. Oh, we talked a lot about you, about The Haven, all kinds of things. He can be quite persuasive, you know.'

I did know. I knew, too, that Faye would quickly ingratiate herself as far as she could into his confidence.

'I've already heard some of this from Hugh,' I told her. 'Look, Faye — what you did to me, that's one thing, but I thought you really cared about The Haven. And especially about Lowell. So why did you — '

'Why did I try to stab him in the back?' she finished for me. Her eyes avoided mine, but she was obviously so shaken by events that she needed to wipe the slate clean. 'You're very naive. Because I felt he'd stabbed me in the back, why else?

'I was furious with him, if you must know. I gave up a good job to help him with The Haven and — well, just to be near him. He kept me at arm's length, then, when he started paying attention to you, it was too much to swallow. Now there's an admission for you.'

There was bitterness in her voice,

and I realised how great an effort the words cost.

'And all the while our fascinating Dr M has a wife and a son tucked away in Italy — and I never knew!' she added.

'I knew,' I said simply.

She looked at me then, astounded, mortified, and angered. This conversation was altogether too painful for both of us. I took no pleasure in her distress.

'Well, thanks for letting me know, but it's all past history now.' I told her. 'Please give me all the latest news. I feel as if I've slept for years.'

There was plenty to hear. Mostly the news concerned Lowell's present hasty trip to Italy — at a vastly inconvenient time, unless, in fact, he welcomed escape as I had welcomed it yesterday. A sudden SOS had come from the Moroni home. There had been an accident. In a remote mountain area, their car had skidded off the road, just at the beginning of their holiday.

'That's why I'm rushing him to the airport,' Faye explained. 'He attracts drama like other people attract midges on a summer night. Have you noticed? It isn't clear how serious the accident was, but I know his grandfather was injured.'

Faye was getting to her feet, with the relief of a duty done.

'And the boy, and Mrs Moroni?' I asked.

'They were all taken to hospital. He'll tell you, you'd better ask him. Oh, before I go — I was to give you these.' She retrieved the wrapped flowers which she had set down on entering. 'From Hugh. He told me what to buy.'

'Then you've seen Hugh? I thought he wasn't seeing anyone.'

'He isn't.' She didn't elaborate on how she had got through the defences. 'He couldn't manage a pen — he was very lucid, but very tired — and he also told me the message. With all his love, he said.'

I glimpsed inside the wrapper a spray of exquisite cream and apricot roses nestling among feathery fern.

'It was kind of you to bring them. And, Faye, thank you for telling me everything.' I said.

She nodded, not waiting for any more. Plainly she wanted nothing more than to get away from me. 'I'll call Lowell, he wants to see you alone, too.'

I went on sitting there on my bed, carefully pulling aside the paper to see and hold those very beautiful flowers. I thought of Hugh, in all his pain and turmoil, choosing them for me. I thought of the last words he had said to me, in love and tenderness.

'Hi! And how's Mrs Hastings today?' a voice said then.

I felt my face flush crimson. It had only been moments since I'd looked through the window and understood fully my longing for Lowell.

I said shakily that I was well. I watched him come in, not cushioned upon purring wheels, but as I had seen him on many evenings, labouring with fierce determination up and down The Haven's grounds. Now, like then, his hair was damp upon a brow creased and heated with triumphant effort.

'How about this?' he asked breathlessly. 'Next week I'll dump these damn crutches and go jogging.'

'And the best of luck,' I said. His eyes were still tired, but he looked very much better than my last glimpse of him, surveying in exhaustion his crumbled dream.

'So you have your flowers.' He sat down where Faye had sat, with a grunt of relief. 'But not much recompense for the way Hugh Egerton has treated you.'

As usual, he put my own half-formed thoughts into stark words. He leaned towards me, his voice very quiet. 'We know Hugh is the tall handsome hero everyone loves to love. If he trades on the image, well, OK, it's for all the best reasons. But underneath he's just like the rest of us. He's only human. And all of us poor humans can fall apart when the going gets rough. We all have things in our lives we remember with shame and hope will be forgiven us — so why not give the guy a break?'

I laid the roses down quite suddenly, with an odd sense of guilt for having held and caressed them. 'Oh, I told him I'd forgiven him! What do you take me for? How could I still hold a grudge after he saved Jeremy from the fire?'

'Correction — your sense of logic may have forgiven him, but your heart hasn't.'

To talk about my heart was dangerous. 'I just keep remembering how he screamed when that burning roof started collapsing,' I said. 'It makes my blood run cold.'

'Maybe he's as terrified of fire as you were of water. But you still dived in yesterday for me, and he still went after the boys. That's real courage. Think about it.'

I nodded, but just now I didn't want to think about Hugh. The nearness of Lowell was robbing me of connected thought.

'Tell me about this car accident,' I said quickly. 'Were all of them hurt?'

'Luke and Rita and Cesare — he's the chauffeur — weren't seriously hurt, I believe. Cuts and bruises and shock.' He was frowning now, the lines on his forehead deeper. 'Of course, anything is serious for my grandfather. He's an old man.'

'Exactly! Didn't I tell you that before, and beg you to end the quarrel? But, no, you had to be so proud and bitter, it's taken this to get you started! Lowell, you're so good at preaching — and so bad at practising!'

Although I spoke harshly, his pain was my pain and I ached to comfort him. I heard him give a weary and troubled sigh.

'Well, I'm on my way now, I'll be with them tonight. There's not too much to keep me in England any more. But I couldn't go without thanking you for all you did at The Haven. I'm sorry your job ended so quickly. You were doing very well.'

This time I couldn't trust my voice to answer. He had to go, and I wanted him

314

to stay. It was hard to see anything beyond that.

'Yes, you did well. We'd really started to get our act together — only Hugh's 'campaign' would probably have broken it up, anyway,' he was saying. 'But I'd have made a good fight of it!' He was still looking straight into my face. 'In case you wondered, the allegation about the child who died back in the States was true. Poor little Marty Donohough. Due to a member of my staff whom I dismissed on the spot.'

'I knew you weren't to blame!'

'Did you? Hugh's other trump card — the misappropriation of funds — was also true.'

'Oh! It — it was?'

'Uh-huh. Let's say I borrowed a sum to pay for a new spinal operation for one of the kids. I figured I could always pay it back later. But, of course, the deficiency came to light before I could return the money. The operation proved unsuitable, it never took place.

It was all a disaster.'

He shrugged expressive shoulders. 'I've been told I have an accommodating conscience, it gets me into a heap of trouble. But I meant no harm — like our two young arsonists in the tower with their candles. Only — now the second Haven has gone the way of the first. So that's the finish.'

'I'm so sorry.' The words seemed trite and inadequate. I struggled to find others. 'But surely this doesn't have to be the end? Haven't you always driven us all crazy insisting anyone can do anything if they really try?'

If he understood the depth of my caring, he didn't heed it. He just shook his head.

There was a sound at the door then and Faye looked in, her face expressionless, to say time was pressing.

Not just pressing, I thought. It had already run out.

★   ★   ★

'Kevin, watch it, that's the cup with the crack!' Penny hissed under her breath, whisking it away. 'I'm sorry the flat's such a mess, everyone, but what with dashing down to Cornwall and having Paula back home so suddenly . . . '

'Don't worry about it,' Faye said with the condescension that had always riled me.

'Mess? What mess?' Lowell asked. 'I call this lived in. Comfortable! OK?'

'OK,' Penny assented delightedly. She seemed to find his powerful personality quite fascinating, and in this brief pause for refreshments was chattering to him like a long-lost friend. In her faded jeans and T-shirt, her coppery ponytail bobbing, she looked about 15 years old. In the background, the bearded Kevin amiably dispensed cups and plates.

I still couldn't quite believe in this scene; Lowell sitting in this familiar room drinking coffee and answering questions. It was wonderful, he agreed, that I was so well again. He hoped I would find another chance to utilise my skill with sick children. No, he hadn't seen Hugh, but Faye could testify to all the flowers and cards that were arriving at the Penvor Hospital in cartloads.

'Tubby and Cuddles,' I mumbled foolishly. 'What happened to them eventually?'

'Good grief, are they patients or staff?' Penny asked.

'More trouble than either,' Lowell explained gravely. Our furry friends, he assured me, along with our scaly ones in the tank, were installed at Debbie's mother's guest house in St Owen; excepting Cleopatra, who was at present on the loose.

In the midst of this, Faye tapped his arm and pointed to her watch. But at the door there was further delay. Jeremy was just coming in as they were going out.

He had arrived from upstairs with his crony, Adam. Beside him, Jeremy looked pale and heavy-eyed, his damaged arm in a sling. At any other time he would have been immensely proud to show off so interesting an injury. Now, suddenly face to face with Lowell, he became paler still in apprehension.

'Hi, how are you guys doing?' Lowell hailed the boys. 'How's the arm, Jeremy?'

'It hurts. It's all stiff. I have to keep seeing the doctor.'

'Tough luck. So you wouldn't be hitting any home runs for the Bears?'

The allusion to those early-morning ball games, now only a memory, seemed to upset Jeremy still more.

'Or lighting any more candles, I hope?' Lowell added quietly.

Penny and Kevin were ahead in the hall with Faye and Adam's mother, all deep in conversation. There was no witness but me, in whom Jeremy had already confided, and Adam, who shuffled nervously beside his friend. I saw that Lowell had touched the right chord. It brought Jeremy's pent-up guilt and remorse tumbling out.

'Oh, I never meant to start that awful

fire! Tony and me, we never meant to! And I wish The Haven hadn't burned down and people hadn't been hurt. I just wish and wish I could go back to before it happened and not do it!'

'I know the feeling,' Lowell acknowledged. 'Sorry, Jeremy, we can't ever do that. We're saddled with what we do, and the consequences, for keeps.'

I put out a protective hand towards Jeremy, then drew it back. He had to brave this out for himself.

'Come on now,' Lowell rallied him. It was his hand that tilted up the boy's chin then ruffled the spiky, red hair. 'You've been honest, you're really sorry and that's the most important thing. Here's what you must do. Sit down and write a long letter to Mr Egerton. I'm sure Adam here will help you. Explain how you feel and how you hope he gets well soon, and thank him for — oh, you'll know what to say.'

'I will?' Jeremy quavered. 'Yes, I will.'

'And don't go on worrying yourself sick over a mistake you can't alter. Start over again, OK?'

The boys went in and we went out. The front door was open, the others were waiting outside. But I held Lowell back one moment more.

'Thank you for that. Very, very much. And when you get to your family, I hope the news is good. I'll be thinking of you . . . ' I struggled with more words. 'And, Lowell, remember what you said to me, 'too late' are the saddest words ever? It mustn't happen to you like it happened to me. You've healed so many people's lives, now just think of your own.'

I wasn't sure if his eyes had misted. For a moment I thought so.

From the doorway, Faye called, 'Are you coming, Lowell?'

'Bless you, Paula. Be happy.' Just those brief words were my farewell, no touch, no smile. 'I'm so glad I could give you back your memory. I'm glad at least one of my screwball schemes worked out.'

Blindly, I turned back into the room,

wanting to see and hear no more. I was aware after a moment that Penny and Linda had drifted in and were handing out the remaining cakes to the boys and Linda's little girl.

'One of my schemes worked out,' Lowell had just said. 'You got back your memory, one of my screwball schemes worked out . . . '

It was like a lightning flash of revelation, appalling, beyond belief. I ran out of the flat like a mad thing, uncaring what anyone thought. By a miracle, Faye's grey car was still at the kerb. Another driver had boxed her in, so an irritated Faye and a helpful Kevin had gone in search of the offender.

I pulled open the car door. 'All right, there's something I've got to know,' I said fiercely. 'Did you throw yourself in that horrible pool deliberately, or didn't you? You're not leaving till you've told me the truth, not if I have to sit down in front of this car!'

If my memory was restored, so, too, was the old fire of my nature. I saw anger now in his face. 'Why must you be so damn clever?' he muttered. 'All right, you've guessed it — I didn't fall. I wanted you to go through the same trauma as when Robert was drowned. And it worked, didn't it?'

'You took a terrible risk like that? You in your physical condition! Suppose I hadn't been a good enough swimmer to save you? And I almost didn't, you very nearly drowned, don't you realise that? And — and — ' I trailed off. 'Don't you know if you'd died I — I should have died, too?'

Somehow I had hold of his hand. Just for a moment its grip on mine was hard and warm and strong.

'But you did save me,' he said simply. 'It was a gamble worth taking. For you it was, Paula.'

That was all. Faye was already hurrying back with the driver of the other vehicle. Soon her way was clear, and the car shot away up the street. I was left standing on the pavement, waving my hand.

In a daze I wondered if it was possible that he had for me even a little of the love I had for him? Even that perhaps he cared for me enough to give his life in making me well? Whatever the answer, even deeper was my own bright and shining love for this complex, difficult man with all his human failings, with his overriding courage, with his deep compassion for all who erred and suffered.

But it must stay a secret love, a love unspoken. Our two ways lay far apart.

★ ★ ★

It would do me a world of good, people said, to stay at home and rest. I had been ill and under a great strain. Now I must take things very quietly and get back my strength.

For a couple of days I let Penny fuss around me, phoning me continually from work, waiting on me every moment she was home.

On the third day, I decided this was

becoming unendurable. I had already scanned the newspapers, still carrying the odd photo and paragraph about Hugh. There were reports too that the world famous singer Guilio Moroni and his family were recovering well, back at his own home. It just gave a few details, but it was all I needed to know.

Now, Jeremy and I sat together staring glassily at the TV screen; after life at The Haven the empty inactivity of the flat seemed to be affecting him as much as it was me. Adam, of course, was at school. Jeremy couldn't risk riding his bike one-armed. Even the delight of not being able to wash properly was palling.

'Jeremy,' I said suddenly. At least this passive interlude had brought us much closer, which pleased and helped me a great deal. 'I've been thinking . . . '

He glanced round at me. 'I'd like to go back to Cornwall. To see Hugh, of course, and to look at The Haven. You know, it might be possible to start the place up again, it just might be.'

'But it was all burned,' Jeremy told me seriously. 'You know it was.'

'I don't know all of it was. The tower wing, of course, and some of the debris fell through another roof, and there was the smoke damage, and the water — oh yes, it's a mess. But messes can be cleared up sometimes. And if I could get other people interested, before all the staff and the children settle down elsewhere . . . Well, it may be just a daydream, but I can't sit here doing nothing!'

He gazed at me. He might be forgiven for thinking my senses were wandering again.

'Of course,' I hurried on, 'if I go, you don't have to come, too. You can stay here with Aunt Penny, and Adam's mum will have you when she's out — and soon you'll be able to go back to school with Adam . . . ' I trailed off, aware of the lack of enthusiasm in his face.

At this vital point, the phone interrupted us. It would either be

Hugh's secretary or Hugh himself, with twice daily greetings from Cornwall, or else another of Penny's calls. In fact, it was Penny.

Her excited voice flooded forth. 'Oh, Paula, love — are you all right? Oh, I'm just back from lunch.'

'From lunch? It's past three!'

'I know, but no one minded when I explained. You see, I met Kevin for lunch, and — and we're getting married! We're engaged! Kevin wasn't eating his burger and chips, and he usually wolfs them down, you know, then he suddenly asked me . . . '

'Well, that's marvellous,' I said warmly. 'I like Kevin a lot.'

'Do you? Oh, I'm so glad you do. Of course, we shan't have a wonderful fairy tale wedding like yours and Hugh's is going to be, but I don't care. Paula,' she rushed on, 'I never really thought he'd ask me, I thought he was married to his bike!'

'And his beard?' I prompted. Again I told her when I could get a word in, how genuinely pleased I was. I told her, too, that I had some staggering news of my own. Perhaps, indeed, it was the thought of Penny's reactions to losing me again so soon that had kept me passive this long. Now, she had far too much on her mind to care greatly about this mad impulse of mine.

'Listen,' I tried to calm her, 'I feel fine, and I'm going back to Cornwall to see if there's enough left of The Haven to open it up again. Do you understand?'

It took her a while. She said I was crazy, of course. 'You might do it if Hugh helped,' she said then. 'And he will, isn't it right up his street?'

'Is it?' I said.

'Of course! Saving good causes when they're almost lost — that's his trademark.'

I didn't mention that recently Hugh had tried to smash this particular good cause.

When finally I put down the phone, I turned to an interested Jeremy.

'She's marrying him then?' he asked. 'Do you think when he's my uncle he'll let me ride on the back of his bike?'

'Maybe,' I said guardedly. 'Let's rush to the shops and buy them a nice engagement present. Then I have to start packing. I'm leaving early tomorrow.'

'Mmm — ' He rubbed a freckled nose. 'Mum, if you're really going, couldn't I go with you and help? So long as we don't have to eat any more of old Ma Burns' super-yukky semolina puddings!'

'Not one.' I guaranteed. 'And I'm sure you could help me a lot.'

On the way to the door I heard his somewhat subdued, 'Yippee!' Subdued, yes, but infinitely better than no yippee at all.

★　★　★

The weather was on my side, the days were golden and glorious, the sea was blue as sapphire and green as turquoise.

Not that I had much chance to enjoy it. From the moment of my arrival back in St Owen, welcomed warmly in Debbie's parents' guest house, I seemed to step upon a treadmill of work, worry, effort and energy that never let up.

If I had still any doubts about asking Hugh for help, I found at our first reunion — still in his room at the Penvor Hospital, where he had chosen to stay for the present — that there was no need to ask. One hint about my project was enough.

'You can have a blank cheque, Paula. Do whatever you want. I can pull a lot of official strings. We'll get Jan in on it, she's a wonder.'

He was sitting out in a chair now, a little more each day. He still looked a shadow of himself. It needed no effort to be very kind to him, to accept his eager help which he so clearly wanted to give.

So that was Janet Fisher — his frighteningly capable secretary in dark-rimmed spectacles and business-like, tailored suits — instantly enrolled. Another eager helper was Debbie, always ready to keep an eye on Jeremy, post letters, run errands, and make tea. But perhaps my greatest ally, my unlikeliest partner, was Faye Prescott. She had been handling the situation here unaided, staying on in the district to deal with correspondence and so on, passing just an occasional item on to Lowell.

'You're in touch with him?' I said quietly the day I arrived.

'Oh, yes. I had a note today, it just says the invalids are progressing.'

'He doesn't say anything about coming back?'

'Not a word. Why?' she asked me directly.

'Because — while he's still away, I want to try getting The Haven started up again. Oh, I know you'll think I'm still mad . . . '

For a moment her brow wrinkled in thought. 'But why not? You know, I was down there this morning looking round and I was thinking . . . Come on, jump in the car and I'll show you!'

She didn't ask me, 'Do you think this will get him back?' The question hung heavily in the air between us, unasked and unanswerable.

Whether we were truly mad or maybe just ostriches with our heads in the sand, we made a good team. With Hugh's liberal financing and string-pulling, there were soon all sorts of vans pulling up at The Haven site — survey-ors, builders, a firm of cleaners who did 'major blitz jobs.' The vans' occupants all began by shaking their heads. It didn't get them far. I found myself, as leader of the project because it was my idea, refusing to take no for an answer, bulldozing through arrangements in a manner worthy of Lowell himself.

Essentially, the ruined tower must be boarded up, made safe, isolated for future rebuilding at some later time. The other end of the building must be made habitable, a reduced-size Haven ready for a reduced-size list of patients

— if we could entice anyone back.

Spoiled curtains and carpets had to be stripped and replaced, along with furniture and linen and everything else. Ignore the cost, Hugh said, so I cheerfully did. There were the insurance people to talk to, the Health and Safety people, and all sorts of others. There were letters and phone calls, interviews and shopping trips. Also, grubby, down-to-earth sorting and salvaging.

During those glowing summery days, I worked 14-hour shifts. In deplorable old jeans and a baggy shirt I was mostly around The Haven, leaving Faye to sally elegantly forth to do most of the replacement shopping. She had, of course, excellent taste.

As soon as I could use Lowell's office for my headquarters, all of us had frequent meetings there. Jan Fisher, armed with files of correspondence, Faye with shopping catalogues, Debbie with endless trays of tea — and Jeremy, so eager to help, busy producing notes in wobbly writing to all The Haven children. He was inviting them to our Grand Re-opening Party.

'We're winning, guys!' Faye greeted us one day with a smile. 'Just keep up with The Haven spirit, one hundred per cent effort! Isn't that right, Paula?'

I agreed, and choked back an urge to ask if she had heard again from Lowell. I couldn't let her see how I lived for those brief and distant notes he sent. She probably knew, anyway.

'I suppose you do realise we may be wasting our time and making complete fools of ourselves?' she said to me later, when we were alone. 'He may already have decided to stay put in Italy — and who could blame him! It's taking a lot for granted to assume he'll agree to live here in a clinic full of our difficult kids.'

It was a devastating viewpoint.

'If he doesn't want to continue The Haven, at least now that'll be his own choice, not a decision forced on him,' I answered quietly.

Faye grunted at that cool, calm logic. Really, of course, I wasn't cool or calm. I was doing this thing because I had sworn to myself it must be done and, meantime, each day I sat a while with Hugh. He was slowly getting back on his feet.

Truly, I was grateful beyond words for his help with The Haven. Day after day, I kept thinking in a numb, resigned fashion that once the resurrected Haven was handed back to Lowell I would be free, quite free. No doubt, then, a long, quiet honeymoon would help Hugh and help me to recover together from all we had been through.

I hadn't told him this in so many words, but nor had I said otherwise. It would be cruel in the extreme to let things go on this way, unless deep down my decision was formed. This was going to be my future, dedicated to Hugh and all his valuable work. So the diamond that glittered somewhere deep in that eerie pool might just as well be still on my finger.

'Oh, Paula.' Faye hailed me with unconvincing casualness early on the

Friday preceding our reopening. 'Do you want the good news or the bad news? I just spoke to Lowell on the phone . . . '

'Tell me the worst,' I said. 'He's guessed, and he wants nothing to do with it?'

'Wrong. He hasn't guessed, and he's coming tomorrow. I told him it was vitally important and he was needed. He said, 'OK, we'll be here by two' — which will be just in time for the party. Of course,' she explained flatly, 'he doesn't know yet it's a party. His idea is to return to Italy the next day.'

I nodded. I repeated carefully, 'He said 'We'll be here'? Who is 'we'?'

'Ah. He didn't make that clear, but it looks obvious to me. He's really coming here to ask the orphanage people for a new offer on the premises — and Rita Moroni is tagging along to make quite sure he accepts it. What do you think?'

'Maybe you're right,' I told Faye briskly, 'but standing gossiping here won't help us.'

Perhaps, I thought later, it would be a good thing if Rita did come. A living flesh and blood Rita, to exorcise the last of my dreams.

★ ★ ★

A breeze from the sea dallied with several dozen brightly-coloured balloons strung around the newly-painted entrance. In pride of place was a large banner made from a sheet, proclaiming in huge letters, WELCOME BACK TO THE HAVEN!

'A waste of good bed linen if ever I saw one,' Mrs Burns said dourly.

I had been amazed, when I doubtfully approached the housekeeper, to find her ready to come back — of course, with the proviso, 'just till you find someone permanent.' As she came, naturally Joe came too. The yellow mini-bus was back in business, and all morning the worried little man had been painstakingly cutting the grass, while a familiar Haven 'path sweeping detail' of children was led by Jeremy.

I couldn't welcome Morgan warmly enough when he was delivered to us by his mother — a plump, pouting woman — clearly unwilling to part with him. He had flatly insisted on returning. His mother admitted cagily that she found him improved. She didn't stay for the ceremony.

Morgan still resembled a barrel in too many clothes and full-moon glasses, but it seemed to me his brave work during the fire, and all the consequent praise, had changed him greatly for the better.

Altogether, we had rounded up seven children. A sprinkling of parents were present, and all of them expressed their surprise and pleasure in finding, over the past couple of weeks, the improvements our regime had achieved. Mrs Beecher was back, too, just arrived, and lost in admiration at the rapid restoration job.

'I don't believe this. It's all going too well,' Faye murmured to me.

She hurried off then to receive the guest of honour, as a taxi turned in at the gates. Hugh had come for a couple of hours from the hospital, insisting he couldn't miss this occasion. It was Faye who helped him to a seat on the lawn — and who bent beside him to smile for the photographers from the Press. I didn't really object.

Of course, a knot of people gathered quickly around the still-scarred and limping Hugh: Sophie, Bridget's aunt, Ben's parents, even Mrs Burns. Well, with Hugh it would always be so.

I stood there with the children lined up and waiting, reassuring Bridget, who held a presentation bouquet in her misshapen hands. Now this moment had come, my legs turned to rubber. I heard the St. Owen church clock strike two. As though in answer, a second taxi turned up the drive.

'Lowell, how are you?' Faye's clear, composed voice said. Inevitably, another voice said, 'Hi, there!' Then, I

339

looked up. With Lowell was a raven-haired boy, who had already taken a pair of crutches from the boot and was now carefully helping his father out of the car. Startlingly, I was looking at a young, tall, active version of Lowell himself. There came to me the lightning remembrance of an evening slide-show when Lowell accidentally flashed a family group on to the screen.

Lowell and Luke were the only ones in the car. For one instant, across the colourful, crowded scene, my eyes met Faye's.

I heard Lowell's gasp as he surveyed for the first time the bobbing balloons and the banner and the assembled crowd — and most of all, the patched-up bulk of The Haven in a triumphant shimmer of new paint. As Bridget crept up to him with her offering of flowers, he gazed at her like a man in a dream.

People were clamouring around him. 'Isn't it wonderful?' and 'Isn't it a lovely surprise?' and 'It was Paula's idea!' My reception committee had disintegrated suddenly into chaos.

Mrs Beecher pushed her way forward. 'Now tell us what you think of the grand transformation.'

Lowell still didn't tell us. For one moment I thought in horror that he was going to burst into tears. I was utterly shaken, furious with myself for doing things this way. But that dominating will of his, by an almost visible effort, quickly restored him enough to smile into the eager faces and clasp the extended hands.

'Bridget, come here, honey,' he called to the child who was backing uneasily away. 'You did that beautifully. I wouldn't have taken the flowers from anyone else but you.'

Bridget beamed, but I saw Luke close at his side making urgent inquiries in soft, voluble Italian. Lowell answered him in the same language. I was glad the boy was so anxious, I was more than thrilled the two of them seemed so close and so caring.

'Paula.' Lowell got round to me at last. 'Well, I don't know what to say . . . '

He didn't need to say anything. I looked into his eyes, into the boy's strained face. I must have been blind not to see the truth at once.

'Shall we go inside, everybody?' I began briskly marshalling the crowd. 'Mrs Burns has provided refreshments in the dining-room, we don't want any left over. Faye, will you look after things?' I asked her. Her brows rose, but she was soon gracefully rounding up stragglers.

'Jeremy — and you, Morgan — I've a special job for you two,' I called to them. 'This is Dr Moroni's son, Luke, he's a stranger here, so will you look after him very specially for me?'

The three boys turned towards the house. 'Come on,' I said to Lowell tersely. I didn't need to persuade him. The sound of his crutches followed me into the leafy concealment of the shrubbery. I sat on the wooden bench and gazed into his face — then suddenly, silently, I caught him in my arms and held him close.

I felt him trembling against me. I heard him sob in the quiet of the garden.

'She died early yesterday. Oh God, why did she have to die!'

'Lowell,' I breathed. I cradled him closer, with a living warmth of human contact that was all I could give. 'Oh, I'm so very, very sorry. But I thought she was getting well after the accident?'

'She was. At first. But . . . ' He choked, holding on to me now with a grip almost painful.

'Tell me. Try to tell me,' I whispered.

Broken, half-coherent, gradually the words came. Indeed, it wasn't the accident alone that killed Rita, still so young, still so beautiful. She was fatally ill before the delayed shock and the quite minor injuries had brought on a collapse that hastened her end. For more than a year she had received treatment for a rare blood disorder. The treatment was only partly holding it in check. She hadn't been expected to live much beyond another year.

And Lowell, her estranged husband, had never been told. Due to his past attitude, no one had thought he would really care. It was the greatest, deepest hurt.

But Rita had wanted him beside her in her last hours. Through that last long night he hadn't left her bedside — and finally she had died peacefully in his arms. The destroying bitterness of years melted away, as her fragile hold on life also melted.

He kept repeating now those same sad words, 'Too late, it was too late.' Tears unashamedly flooded his eyes. 'It was too late. We'd wasted all our time . . .'

'I know. I do know. I loved Robert, too, there was so much we could have shared.' In all my tenderness and longing and sorrow, I held his tear-wet face against my own. 'But listen to me, Lowell, try not to grieve too much, try

344

not to break your heart because at least you did say goodbye to her, at least she knew in the end that you'd loved her. I wish Robert had known.'

He didn't answer me. I was crying, too, for his loss and for mine. And yet, in the midst of all this pain, I knew one glimmer of joy; that he was clinging to me for help in this darkest of hours.

'Lowell.' I struggled to reach him, as once, in my own desolation, he had reached me. 'You still have your work to do. Oh, it may not seem important now, but it will again. And you have Luke; he needs you now so badly. And your grandfather is old and alone.' I didn't add that he had me, my undying devotion for always. This wasn't the right moment. Would there ever be a right moment?

'Come on.' I rallied him more sternly now. I even shook him a little, like an obstinate child. 'The world's still going on. So are you going to sit back and wallow in self-pity — or are you going to look after the children, who need you to bully them and coax them and start them living again? Oh, you won't ever get over this, but you'll learn to live with it. You have the strength to begin again. And the strength to help so many other people begin again.'

It was at that instant some sound came to me. A movement, a footstep, I wasn't sure just what it was. I looked up, my face still wet with tears, my arms still holding the man I loved so dearly. I knew we were no longer alone.

Hugh's eyes met mine. He stood there with sunlight dappling his pale face. However much he had seen and heard, it had been enough.

'Please, don't move. I'll only intrude a moment.' His voice was quite steady. 'I just wanted to say — I've been speaking to Luke and I'm very sorry. There's something else I must say; it's high time I left here. Jan can fix me up in a convalescent home nearer London, then I'll start thinking about work . . . '

'Hugh,' I said shakily. 'Wait, I — I can explain.'

'You don't have to explain anything. I've been deluding myself. It was foolish of me.' He gave me a smile that was sad and kind. 'Paula, don't look so worried. I'll see you again before I leave for London. We'll sort things out. And if ever I can help you, just ask.'

He was already turning away. Momentarily I sat there turned to stone; at that moment I was only deeply sorry for Hugh, so fine and good a man. If that goodness was flawed, who in the wide world was perfect? The words he hadn't spoken now meant so much more than those he had. He loved me, but he accepted my heart wasn't his — and so quietly, without bitterness, he was withdrawing from my life. Could many have done as much?

When I hurried after him, I saw his taxi still waiting on the drive. As the driver opened the door, Faye materialised from nowhere. The thought flashed into my mind that they made a fine-looking couple. When Hugh returned to his busy, colourful life he would get over losing me, but he would need someone.

So, good luck, Faye, I thought silently.

'Oh, Paula, dear.' Mrs Beecher bustled up to me. 'We're waiting to drink the toast, where has Dr Moroni vanished to?'

'I'll tell him you're waiting,' I said.

★   ★   ★

The toast to a new Haven was drunk in tea, coffee, lemonade, or anything that came to hand. I watched, in the bright, crowded room, as Lowell gamely made his way round to shake a hand here, exchange a comment there, while the children clamoured round explaining who had made the ginger cookies or decorated the fish tank with crepe paper.

He made a short speech to thank all who were responsible for the renovation job. His eyes were shadowed, his face a little flushed.

While he was speaking, Faye slipped back into the room, her face a shade more flushed than his. Hugh apologised for leaving early, she reported, but he was feeling rather tired.

'Sorry, Lowell,' she added, 'for interrupting.'

'I've really finished. I just have to say, I'm going back to Italy with Luke tomorrow for a little spell — but I'll be back. If you guys need me here, although it hardly looks as though you do!' His voice was suddenly serious, and he looked at me. 'I've a lot of new plans. All sorts of plans. But I need a little time first . . . '

I knew he wasn't speaking only about The Haven. We both needed time. Time, and the healing of time.

A little later, from the end of the dining-room, we watched together with mutual pleasure the raven-haired Luke and the flame-haired Jeremy side by side, deep in conversation.

Lowell's eyes lingered on the group of Haven children who had posed such varied problems. 'You were right, of course, Paula. What you told me just now. And I'm wondering, if I get my grandfather over here soon on a visit — he has far more lire tucked away than he knows what to do with — it might be a pushover to persuade him to finance Project Haven Three. Thanks to you, there's still something left to show him and convince him it's worthwhile. I still don't know how in heaven's name you did what you did.'

'Was it really so much to do for you, after you risked your life for me?'

'Ah. Well. The Maiden's Pool.' He looked embarrassed. 'There's something I should tell you about that. Even my conscience does have its limits.'

I watched as he pulled out a little gold medallion which I had often noticed round his neck. He held it out and I read its inscription — a date, the name Lowell Guilio Moroni — and beneath, OUTRIGHT WINNER, PARAPLEGIC SWIMMING CHAMPIONSHIP, NEW YORK.

'Then — you weren't drowning at all?' I exploded. 'So I was really in far more danger in that horrible pool than you ever were?'

'Sorry. Only you were safe enough, really. I've a diploma for life-saving, too.' Momentarily that warm, magical, magnetic smile lighted up his face. 'OK, it was a dirty trick. But I made it all look good. Didn't I make it look good?'

He was laughing and suddenly I was laughing, too. Well, life with him would always be like this. Tears and laughter, tempests and storms, exhausting work and transcending courage. I should be used to it by now.

I went quietly round to talk to Jeremy and Luke and across the bright room I looked again into the saddened blackness of Lowell's eyes, the caring, vulnerable soul beyond. There was a time to reap and to sow, to live and to die. For us, this was a time to grieve. But there would come a time for us to love, to find our new rejoicing.

And it will come, Lowell, my dearest, my eyes told his silently. It will come.

THE END

Other titles in the
Linford Romance Library:

THREE TALL TAMARISKS

Christine Briscomb

Joanna Baxter flies from Sydney to run her parents' small farm in the Adelaide Hills while they recover from a road accident. But after crossing swords with Riley Kemp, life is anything but uneventful. Gradually she discovers that Riley's passionate nature and quirky sense of humour are capturing her emotions, but a magical day spent with him on the coast comes to an abrupt end when the elegant Greta intervenes. Did Riley love Greta after all?

FiEL

'This is a busy practice,' Anna said crisply. 'We work flat out to cater to the needs of the locals, and at this time of year our numbers double because of the tourist population. We don't have time for film crews.'

'But that's the beauty of it,' Polly said cheerfully. 'Sam already knows the score. He's used to being filmed all the time. There'll be very little intrusion, I can assure you.'

'The patients won't like it—'

'The patients will love it,' Sam predicted dryly, lifting a hand and shielding his eyes from the sun. 'And if they don't, they don't have to take part. They always have a right to refuse to be filmed. But I can tell you now that they won't. In fact, I'm willing to bet on it…'

1/06 **Sarah Morgan** trained as a nurse and has since worked in a variety of health-related jobs. Married to a gorgeous businessman, who still makes her knees knock, she spends most of her time trying to keep up with their two little boys, but manages to sneak off occasionally to indulge her passion for writing romance. Sarah loves outdoor life and is an enthusiastic skier and walker. Whatever she is doing, her head is always full of new characters and she is addicted to happy endings.

Recent titles by the same author:

IN THE SHEIKH'S BED
  (Modern Romance™)
THE MIDWIFE'S MARRIAGE
PROPOSAL
  (Medical Romance™)
THE NURSE'S WEDDING RESCUE
  (Medical Romance™)
THE DOCTOR'S CHRISTMAS BRIDE
  (Medical Romance™)
THE GREEK'S BLACKMAILED WIFE
  (Modern Romance™)